Eakins' Mistress

Also by James Bradberry

The Seventh Sacrament
Ruins of Civility

Eakins' Mistress

A Jamie Ramsgill Mystery

James Bradberry

St. Martin's Press ⚓ New York

Library of Congress Cataloging-In-Publication Data

Bradberry, James.
    Eakins' mistress : a Jamie Ramsgill mystery / by James Bradberry.
    —1st ed.
      p.   cm.
    ISBN 0-312-15518-2
    I. Title.
    PS3552.R2127E25   1997
    813'.54—dc21   96-53623
                                                                    CIP

First Edition: May 1997

10 9 8 7 6 5 4 3 2 1

For Louisa and Philippa,
radiance personified

One

*D*avid Laycutt strode through the flock of pigeons near the fountain in the center of Rittenhouse Square, oblivious to the explosive clamor of flight. His mind was focused on completing his firm's drawings for the *Lindenstrasse* competition, which were to be air-shipped to Berlin in little less than ten hours, what would be the culmination of two months' worth of grueling work. As the pigeons flew away, he stepped deftly around George—a scraggly homeless man Philadelphians knew as the Rat Chef, because a local newscast once showed him cooking a rodent in the park.

Laycutt hurried on. He passed a phalanx of elderly ladies, each tended to by a stiff nurse in a pressed white uniform, out on their morning wheelchair strolls, and then two cops sipping coffee from paper cups. On his way out of the park, Laycutt hardly noticed the group of gutter punks on the benches alongside the sidewalk, or the haze of marijuana smoke that hung above them like a neon fog.

Laycutt was absorbed in the world of his own thoughts, unaware of the splendid day. It was early spring and the morning sunlight poked its way between the high-rise apartments on the eastern edge of the square, filtering through the newly unfurled leaves of the sycamores. The park's grass was a vibrant green, and daffodils of pastel yellow dotted the ground like confetti, tossed out in broad, ever-expanding arcs. The air was sharp, though with promise, and many of the park's inhabitants were in shirtsleeves, a few of them lying on blankets in the sun.

At Eighteenth Street, Laycutt picked up his pace, making the light before it turned green. Out of the corner of his eye he caught the steel skeleton of Keystone Place four blocks away, a seventy-five story skyscraper of his own design, now topped out and already dominating the skyline. He hastened past a crowd of slower-moving pedestrians and hopped the curb on the other side of the street. It was there that he came upon Oren Horvitz, a young architect from his office, standing near the old blue newsstand, anxiously waiting for him. Suddenly Laycutt was jerked back into reality. It was Tuesday morning and he was about to face another day in the trenches.

"Morning, Oren," he said, as the young man joined his walk. Like Keystone Place, Laycutt was a mammoth presence, and he towered over Horvitz. At six feet two he was all arms and chest, and his body tapered like a spike. He sensed immediately that the young architect had an item of urgency to discuss.

"David, hi," said Horvitz. It took some effort for Horvitz to keep up with Laycutt's long stride. "I need to see you this morning, if I can, David. About the windows for the Connelly residence. We got the bids, and in bronze, the windows alone were three hundred and twenty thousand dollars."

Laycutt glanced nonchalantly over at Horvitz as the two reached the entrance lobby to their building, just off the square.

"So?" he said, as Horvitz opened the glass door.

"So the whole house is supposed to come in at less than a million. Maybe we should forget bronze and go with wood."

Laycutt pushed the elevator call button, just as the lobby door behind them opened again. A tall woman in a midnight blue suit hurried in, her arms full of rolled-up drawings.

"Oren, please," said Laycutt, motioning toward her.

Horvitz helped her with the load.

"Thanks," she said.

"Morning, Stephanie," said Laycutt.

"Morning," said Stephanie Clark, swinging her thick mahogany brown hair away from her shoulders.

The elevator door opened, the three of them stepped in, and Horvitz pushed the button for the second floor.

"How was the meeting yesterday, Steph?" said Laycutt.

"Terrible. We need to have a conference. Barton says there's no way they can finish construction in time. The client's furious, and they're blaming us because we held up approval of the millwork shop drawings. Their old lease is up in June, and they *have* to get into the new space."

The light above the elevator door lit up, followed by a grating *ding*.

"Okay," said Laycutt. "Let me check my messages. Get Tod and we'll meet in a few minutes."

The trio stepped out into the entry foyer of Laycutt/Farr Architects. Light poured through the enormous windows that faced Walnut Street, warming the white walls and furnishings. A woman with big brown hair was standing behind a curved reception desk, holding a phone to her ear.

"David," she said, bringing the receiver to her chest. "It's Anthony Neville from London. Says it's urgent."

Laycutt nodded, pointing to his right, an indication that he would take the call in his office. Horvitz handed Stephanie Clark her drawings and she left the two men, making her way to the mailboxes behind the reception desk.

"About those windows," said Horvitz, following Laycutt as they walked through a long, high loft space cluttered with work cubicles and abuzz with computers. Jazz and alternative rock simmered on numerous desktop radios. Most of the workers were young, corporate-hip, noses to the grindstone with MTV haircuts.

"Later, Oren," said Laycutt. He couldn't deal with the Connellys' windows on a morning like this. He had a week's worth of work to get done before tomorrow, when he was due to fly to the West Coast for three days. "I'll call Dick Connelly this afternoon. He's going to have to increase the budget."

Horvitz stopped in his tracks, having heard the word from on high. Laycutt continued on through the office.

"David?"

The firm's bookkeeper, Margo Baines, a shapely black woman in a gold silk blouse, called to him from her cubicle. "Are you going to be in all day?"

Laycutt paused, noticing a group of four more architects outside his glassed-in office, waiting for him like vultures.

"I'm afraid so."

"Good," she said authoritatively, her eyes quickly returning to her work. "Remember, I need you for payroll and we also have to talk with Tod about renewing the line of credit."

Laycutt nodded, as if he cared. Payroll and lines of credit held about as much interest for him as foreign policy or stamp collecting. When he became an architect three decades ago, he never once dreamed that when he reached the pinnacle of his profession, he would be haunted by payroll and lines of credit. Those kind of things were supposed to be Tod Farr's problems.

"Good morning," said the four architects outside his door in unison, as if they were quadruplets. In effect, they were. They were the team for the Berlin competition, and Laycutt was sure that they were there to assault him with questions. It had been only nine hours since he had last met with them, just before midnight, upon his return from an evening of entertaining an out-of-town client.

Each of them was wearing ruffled clothes, evidence of an all-night *charette*, and though it was doubtful that any of them had slept last night, Laycutt found it hard to believe that they could be as fatigued as he was. He was on autodrive, but he felt as though his tank was almost empty.

"I've got to just take this call," he said, brushing through the group, making his way into his cluttered office. He ripped off an Armani overcoat and set his briefcase on the floor.

Before him on his black ash desk was a mountain of mail, sorted by his secretary into stacks of *urgent, more urgent,* and *on fire.* He went around to the rear of the desk and picked up the phone. Jamming the receiver between his shoulder and a rather large ear, he thumbed through the correspondence.

"Sir Anthony," he said. "Hello."

The voice from overseas was hollow, but it came bearing good news.

"David, congratulations. The directors have voted to go with you for the new wing of the museum."

Laycutt stopped thumbing, but it wasn't because of what Neville had said. His mind had veered off course. He was staring at a bone-colored envelope, addressed to him. The Jim Thorpe, Pennsylvania, postmark was unmistakable, a postmark that brought back an avalanche of memories. He felt sweat building on his brow, and a black hole in his gut.

"Er . . . what, Anthony?"

4

"The addition, old boy. We've selected your firm."

"Oh," said Laycutt, his voice listless.

"Well, man, you don't sound too excited."

"Oh . . . I am, Anthony. I'm sorry, really, I am. Someone was just talking to me and I was distracted. No, that's great news. Now, look, I've got to run. Sorry."

He lowered the receiver and raised his eyes to the four Apocalyptic horsemen standing at his door. He caught the fact that his jaw was hanging open. He snapped it shut, trying to force a smile.

"I'll be with you guys in a minute," he said, puffing out his cheeks. "I've just got to go to the bathroom first."

He slipped the envelope into the front pocket of his trousers. Back in the open office area, he headed towards the foyer, his mind spinning like a big, unbalanced wheel. He wanted to slap himself, to jar his way out of the nightmare forming before his eyes. A few doors up, he turned left and made his way through the technical library, then past the print room, both of which were under a mezzanine. An architect in the library had her head buried in a furniture catalog, and two young interns were force-feeding the blueprint machine next door, amid sharp fumes of ammonia. He turned left again and, in the short hall that led to the bathrooms, stopped outside the men's room. Just beyond him was a long single-run stair that served as a fire escape, leading to the alley below.

He fished the envelope from his pocket, ripping it open with fingers that were as agitated as popping corn. His breathing was short, and he felt light-headed. Laycutt slipped out a one-page letter and read it, but it was as if the letter was being read by someone else. His eyes glazed over, caroming around the page like a billiard ball, picking up only the most pertinent words and phrases.

He didn't notice the envelope when he dropped it.

Quickly folding the letter and stuffing it back into his pocket, he pushed lightly on the door to the men's room, holding it stationary for a moment. In the reflection of the door's stainless steel push plate, he could see his nearly bald head. His eyes, ringed by dark shadows due to lack of sleep, were wide, looking as though they might literally jump out of their sockets.

Turning back toward the print room, he made sure that he was out of sight of the interns. He let go of the door, which returned to a closed position, the soft hiss of the hydraulic closer followed by silent stillness. He grasped the stair rail, paused for a second, then began a descent of the stair. In thirty seconds he was back out on Eighteenth Street, sweating like the walls of a steambath, without a clue as to what to do next.

Two

*H*ow'd you sleep?" said Cate Chew, who was pouring coffee from a silver Pueforcat coffee service resting on a long pedestal dining table. She looked up to her brother-in-law, Jamie Ramsgill.

"We . . . uh," mouthed Ramsgill in a vacant stare. His eyes circled to Elena Piruzzi, his lover, who was standing before an old painting atop a sideboard. She looked up and Ramsgill caught her exquisite features—the dark silken hair cut short and tucked neatly behind her ears, her straight nose dusted with freckles, and the acute cheekbones, which looked as hard as marble.

"We . . . slept fine," Elena cut in, reaching for the coffee cup Cate held out to her.

Ramsgill laughed to himself. He wondered if Cate knew that he and Elena had hardly slept at all. They had made love, what, three times last night? The first time with ferocity, the second time tenderly, the third in an almost somnambulistic state. They recently had decided to try to have a child, and Elena's time of month had coincided with their visit to Ramsgill's brother's house. As the guest room adjoined Michael and Cate's own bedroom suite, Ramsgill couldn't believe that their nocturnal conduct had gone unnoticed.

"Good," said Cate. She handed Ramsgill his coffee. He looked at her, and the smile she offered led him to believe that she really hadn't heard them last night.

Noticing the flair of the Haviland teacup, he took a sip of hot, strong coffee. It was his first cup of the morning, and it immediately gave him comfort.

"Is this new?" said Elena, looking back at the painting before her.

Ramsgill stepped around the table and joined Elena at the canvas.

They were in the dining room of Michael and Cate's home, a Georgian townhouse in the Society Hill section of Philadelphia. With a high ceiling and well-proportioned egg and dart crown molding, and two pairs of fluted Ionic columns that divided it from the front parlor, the room exuded eighteenth century gentility. The walls were covered with a wallpaper of regimental stripes and adorned with American art. Most of the art was from Philadelphia, ranging from pencil drawings of local landmarks by Joseph Pennell to a large farm scene by the primitivist Horace Pippin.

Michael and Cate were the ideal couple to put together such an environment. Ramsgill's older brother was a partner in the firm of Simpson, Strauss, Kulper and Timberlake, a bastion of Philadelphia law, as well as director of several local corporations and thus had the where-with-all to pursue the finer things in life. Cate was a connoisseur of Americana, particularly from the Federal period. She was assistant curator of American Art at the Philadelphia Museum of Art, with odds of being made a full Curator in the not too distant future. She came from an old, if fractured, Main Line family, and her predisposition for good taste seemed almost genetic.

Ramsgill looked down at the canvas. The painting was two-and-a-half-feet wide and almost as high, set within a simple gilt frame. It was an oil, with a nude woman in the foreground standing *contrapposto* on a block of wood, her body turned partially away from the viewer. She was holding a heavy book on her shoulder, her hips were shifted slightly, one knee extended forward. In the shadowed background of the picture, in the corner of what appeared to be a dark room, was a stout male sculptor in shirtsleeves and a vest, with a hammer and chisel in his muscular hands. He was forming a likeness of the woman out of wood, and there were other wooden sculptures in the foreground, mostly ship scrolls, the kind that adorned seagoing ships in the days of sail and steam. The dress of the characters was late Georgian, but the color palette of earthy browns and sepias more Victorian. The only hint of vibrancy in the painting was the model's skin and clothes, the clothes draped haphazardly over a Chippendale chair in the foreground.

"It's a Thomas Eakins," said Ramsgill.

"It is," said Cate. She joined them in front of the sideboard.

"Is it from the museum?" asked Elena.

"No," said Cate. "I'm authenticating it for a private collector. He's thinking of selling it."

"What's the subject matter?" said Elena.

"It's William Rush," said Cate. She had a salver of toast, and offered some to Ramsgill and Elena. Elena declined but Ramsgill took half a piece.

"Rush was a colonial sculptor," Ramsgill said. "I believe the painting is of him sculpting his allegorical figure of the Schuylkill River. Is that right, Cate?"

"Right. Eakins was thought to have done three versions of the painting in his career. At least until this one came along. There have been rumors of a lost version for years, but like most people, I'd assumed all along that they were just that. Rumors. Even Lloyd Goodrich, who interviewed Eakins' widow in the thirties for his opus on Eakins, made no mention of it."

"You're saying that this is the lost version?" asked Ramsgill.

"Yes."

Cate took a sip of her tea, her green eyes fixed on the canvas.

"A woman named Elinor Addison discovered the painting some twenty years ago," she said. "But it's been a bit of a secret. Addison was a well-known antiques dealer in the city who died recently. She was eighty-seven and something of a legend around town—wired into society, and actually quite good. She had an eagle's eye when it came to Americana."

Ramsgill took a bite of toast, careful not to drop crumbs onto the Empire sideboard.

"So you're authenticating for her estate?" he said.

"Not exactly."

"What do you mean?"

"Well, Mrs. Addison sold the painting about thirteen years ago."

"That must have made her wealthy."

"As a matter of fact," said Cate, "it didn't. See, for some reason Mrs. Addison kept the painting a secret for the first few years she owned it. Then, out of the blue, she had Hayes Chatfield, a curator at the Pennsylvania Academy of the Fine Arts, look at it, as well as a fellow from Christie's in New York."

"And?"

"And they told her it was a fake. Most likely a contemporary forgery."

Ramsgill leaned forward, now studying the canvas more closely. The paint was quite thin over most of the work, the brush strokes of the sepia-toned background almost batiklike. The artist's use of heavier impasto was reserved for the focus of the work, the figures of the model and the sculptor Rush. The figure of the female model was the most striking. She was fully realized in three dimensions, solid and weighty, her pale pink-white skin virtually glowing against the muted brown background. The lines of her body charged the canvas, creating inversions of figure and ground, of dark and light. The canvas was covered with very fine crackleature, a mosaic of small fissures which seemed to denote age. It was signed in the lower right-hand corner, the signature giving no hint that the painting was a forgery. In fact, there was nothing about the painting that construed forgery, though Ramsgill knew that quite often the naked eye can't detect such a thing.

"So how'd they determine it was a forgery?" he said.

Cate smiled, smoothing back her flaming red hair with her right hand.

"I don't know, Jamie," she said. "And that's where things get interesting. Because it *isn't* a fake. I'm sure of that. The pitiful thing is that once the painting was denounced, Mrs. Addison sold it for a few hundred dollars to Harold Farber, the man who brought it to me."

Ramsgill looked over to his sister-in-law.

"Farber's a noted neurosurgeon," Cate continued, as if to answer Jamie's unasked question. "He's also a patron of the arts. In fact, he's on the board of the museum."

"So why is its existence just now coming to light?"

"Farber agreed with Mrs. Addison to not exhibit or sell the painting until she was dead."

"Why?"

Cate shrugged.

"I don't know. Ellie Addison did things her own way. Maybe it was a condition of sale with Farber."

"How are you so sure it's not a forgery?" said Elena, her hand stroking Ramsgill's back.

Cate shifted her gaze to the canvas. It was a probing look, eyes habituated to years of examining works of art.

"I've had a conservator analyze it," she said. "X-ray and chemical analysis. But I'm really depending on intuition. The clincher for me was the depiction of that chair in foreground."

"The one on which the model's clothes are draped?" said Ramsgill. Cate nodded.

"Remember," she said. "The subject of the painting is an event that took place in 1809, even though Eakins' painting is from much later. And Eakins, unlike many of his contemporaries, went to great lengths to be accurate in his work. Some artists would have dressed the figures in contemporary garb, or put in any furniture. But look at the chair. It's a Philadelphia Chippendale chair. It has the distinctive rounded rear legs, instead of square. And even in the painting, though it's quite small, you can see that the chair's side rails are mortised into the chair back, and exposed."

"Which distinguishes it from a Boston chair, or one from New York," said Ramsgill. "But that doesn't prove Eakins himself painted it. A forger could have just copied those details."

"I don't think so, Jamie. I told you that there are other versions of the painting in existence. But in those, there is either no chair, or the chair is turned so that the back isn't visible. And to be sure, I've searched insurance records from Eakins' estate. Eakins owned a pair of such chairs, even described in the records as having that unusual back splat that spreads out at the top and engages the side rails. They were purportedly made by Thomas Tuft, a well-known colonial carver in the city."

"So a forger would have gotten those details wrong?" said Ramsgill.

"I think so. I've also had Aldrich Jacobs of Oberlin College look at the painting and he agrees with me. It *is* an original."

Ramsgill turned and walked around the table to the coffee tray. He poured himself another cup. He was dressed solely in blue. He wore an indigo linen suit with high-cut lapels, a Prussian blue shirt buttoned at the collar, and a vest of a slightly lighter value.

"It must be worth a fortune, then," he said. "Does anything like this ever come up on the market?"

Cate smiled. She was a fine-boned woman slightly younger than Ramsgill's own age of forty-two. She had smooth fair skin and auburn hair, combed back in waves of lighter red. Her eyes were moss green, and they had a naturalness to them that negated a need for makeup.

"Hardly," she said. "A watercolor did come up a few years ago, though. It was a study for one of Eakins' rowing pictures. He had sent it to his teacher in Paris, Gérôme. Gérôme's heirs found it recently. It wasn't really in great shape, but nevertheless it sold for a million three."

"We're talking dollars?"

Cate nodded.

"Then what would this be worth?" said Ramsgill. "I mean, it's an oil as opposed to a watercolor."

"I don't know, maybe six or seven million."

Ramsgill crossed his arms at his chest, rolling his eyes upwards. He made a soft whistling sound.

"Whoa. You've got a pretty good alarm system here, do you, Cate?"

Cate chuckled, joined by Elena, the laughter tumbling off to silence.

"Seriously," said Ramsgill. "Why's it so valuable?"

Cate breathed in a long deep breath, followed by a tightening of her brow.

"It's technically brilliant, for one thing," she said, "the best of all of the Rush series. And there's the mystery of its provenance. How Mrs. Addison found it, then sold it for next to nothing. And historically, it'll be a bombshell."

"A bombshell?" said Elena.

Cate smiled again, this time wryly, the corners of her mouth turned up ever so slightly.

"You're getting a kick out of this," said Ramsgill.

"Let me show you something," she said. She left the room and returned a few moments later with a boxed set of two clothbound books. She slid one of the books out and thumbed directly to a page she seemed to know by heart.

"Here's the first version of *Rush Carving*," she said. "Actually a composition study done in 1875. And here is version two."

She turned the page.

"Done two years later. You can see that the first version has sort of an idealized Greek goddess as the model, which would have been par for the course in Eakins' day. Also, there's the model's chaperone in the picture, off to the right there, looking away from the scene. And the whole composition is rather stilted. But here, in 1877, the painting is much more alive, less romantic. The model for this one was known to be a woman named Nannie Williams, who posed for a number of Eakins' works. This is a real woman, with real flesh and blood, no idealized form. And look at the clothes. Strewn on the chair in the foreground, kind of *in your face* for the Victorian era. In fact a critic for *The New York Times* back then considered the placement of the clothes to be scandalous, saying that they called attention to nudity, which was improper."

Cate again turned through several pages.

"And then there's the one done in 1908," she said. "It's somewhat interesting in that Eakins was known to have used two models for the painting. An older, plain, slightly chunky lady, and a younger, more slender woman. The two of them show up in various studies. But in the final version it's the older woman who is portrayed. Another interesting thing is that the chaperone is now a black woman, a woman known to have worked for Eakins. And Rush himself, who had a slight physique and dressed more like a gentleman, is now portrayed as heavy, and he's wearing a vest, sleeves rolled up. It's pretty clear that Eakins has substituted himself for Rush in this version."

"So let's get back to your bombshell," said Ramsgill.

"Turn around," she said.

They turned away from the book and back toward the painting on the sideboard.

"Give me your assessment of Dr. Farber's version," said Cate. "Knowing what you know now."

They stared silently, then Elena spoke up.

"Well, it seems to portray Eakins again as the sculptor," she said. "He's definitely stout, dressed like a craftsman, not a gentleman."

"Right."

"And the top two buttons of his shirt are unbuttoned," said Ramsgill. "Revealing, shall we say, a *throbbing mass* of chest hair?"

"Don't get pornographic on me," said Cate. "But you're warm."

"The model," said Elena. "It's the younger woman. She's turned more to the side. You can see her breasts now. And . . . " She paused.

"Pubic hair," said Cate. "Right. And what about the chaperone?"

"There is no chaperone," said Ramsgill.

"Touché," said Cate.

"And look at Eakins' eyes."

"They're trained on the model," said Ramsgill. "In every other version they're concentrating on the chisel in his hand."

"So what are you saying, Cate?" asked Elena. "That this woman and Eakins were . . . "

"Judge for yourself," said Cate. "I'll just say that Eakins was a realist. The subjects of his paintings were always reflective of real life. If he painted this woman in a more revealing—I'll even go so far as to say *erotic*—pose . . . then he was portraying a real event."

"Himself in the studio with her," said Ramsgill. "*Sans* chaperone."
Cate nodded.

"When was this one done?" said Ramsgill.

"My guess is sometime just before the 1908 version."

"So Eakins must have been rather old."

"In his late fifties. Or early sixties."

"And the model looks quite young."

"Definitely."

"Was Eakins married?"

"Until the day he died."

"Who was the model?"

"No one knows for sure. William Faircloth, who's a historian at Bennington, surmised it might have been a young woman named Bachman or Backman or something."

"So what we've got is a ninety-year-old scandal. The greatest American figurative painter of the nineteenth century having an affair with his model, preserved for posterity by the painting."

"So it would seem."

"Where did Mrs. Addison get the painting?"

"She supposedly bought it off someone up in the Fairmount area, on a block near to where Eakins himself lived. It had been found in an attic or something. I don't know much about it. Her niece runs her shop now, and there are no records of her having made the purchase."

"That's strange, isn't it?" said Ramsgill. "I mean, I might be stupid, but if you had what you thought was an original Eakins, wouldn't you want as much documentation on it as possible? To try to develop a provenance?"

"You would normally, Jamie. But Mrs. Addison always did things her own way. And you also have to remember that the painting probably never saw the light of day. Eakins would have kept its existence a secret. Which meant that its provenance would have been nonexistent."

Just then a big voice came from the direction of the kitchen.

They turned in unison to see Michael Ramsgill bursting through the dining room door. A cordless telephone was wedged between his ear and left shoulder, and with his free hand he was pushing a watch up his chunky wrist. He barked something to the person on the other end of the line, then said good-bye and set the phone on the table.

He then poured himself a quick cup of coffee, swilling half the cup immediately, wincing at a burned tongue.

"So," he said. "Jamie's big day. A job interview. A real job."

Michael walked over and pecked Cate on the cheek, then kissed Elena. He approached his younger brother and squeezed the shoulder of his suit jacket. He whispered, "Get much sleep last night, brother?"

Jamie cringed. The smirk planted on Michael's square jaw was as wide as the Atlantic. Michael squeezed his shoulder once more for good measure, then walked again to the table, buttering himself a piece of toast.

"So you're finally calling a marker on your old friend, Laycutt," said Michael. "I think that's great, Jamie. And moving back to Philly too. It only took you twenty years to realize that academia was, well . . . what shall we say . . . devoid of meaningful compensation? But once you're working for Laycutt/Farr and making some real money, you'll forget about dear old Princeton."

"Michael," said Cate, "don't be so crude. You couldn't get a teaching position at Princeton if your life depended on it."

"Of course I couldn't," Michael said, stuffing a piece of toast into his mouth. "They don't have a law school, dear."

"He's a Philistine, Jamie," said Cate. "Ignore him."

"I am decidedly not a Philistine," said Michael. "I love art. I just also happen to love making money. So I can buy the art. And I think that Jamie working for one of the best known architecture firms in the country will be great for him. And for his pocketbook."

"First of all," said Jamie. "I haven't been offered a job. Second, I'm not leaving Princeton for the money. I'm leaving because I'm tired of teaching. And Michael, what you don't know about architecture is that there's an inverse relationship between the quality of an architect's work and the financial success of his or her firm. Schlock architects make a ton of money, while someone like David pours all of his profits back into the firm. He's struggled for years to make a name for himself."

"But he's made that name now, Jamie, surely."

"He has. But I can tell you he's not wealthy. And if I go to work for him I'm not going to retire anytime soon."

"You're just like Mother, Jamie. Idealist to the end," he said. "By the way, did I show you this?"

Michael pushed up the French cuff to his shirt. An antique art deco watch, gold with a black face, adorned his wrist.

"Cate gave it to me," he said. "For my birthday. Nine thousand dollars."

Jamie looked over to Cate, who was blushing.

"It's nice," he said. "Very nice."

Michael patted him on the shoulder, in a slightly patronizing way.

"So how about Cate's Eakins?"

"My Eakins?" she said.

"Okay, Farber's," said Michael. "But it's pretty amazing, huh?"

Ramsgill nodded, but already Michael was forging ahead.

"You know, they say that Eakins was technically as gifted as any painter of the nineteenth century, but that he was too conservative. That he couldn't hold a candle to the Impressionists. I think that's rubbish."

"You're probably right," said Jamie. "He——"

"They also say that his subject matter was too mundane," Michael interrupted. "Are you kidding me? The man painted life itself. In all of its glory. In all of its simple routine. Don't you think that's an unwarrantable criticism, Jamie?"

"I suppose——"

"Well," Michael broke in, "I've got to run. I'm handling a merger deal for Merck today. I should have been at the office two hours ago."

He stuffed another piece of toast into his mouth.

"And," he said, walking over to his wife and kissing her again, "I'll be working late tonight."

"Michael," Cate said. "That's two nights in a row. We told Jamie and Elena we'd take them to dinner. I've got reservations at Striped Bass at eight."

"You'll have to go without me," Michael said, shrugging at Jamie, and now heading through the front parlor. "Our deal involves a Japanese company so we'll be burning the midnight oil. You do understand, don't you, brother?"

Jamie started to speak, but before he could, Michael was through the parlor and in the front hall, getting his coat.

"Michael!" cried Cate.

"Sorry," he said, craning his head and popping it back through the open doorway. "Look, really I am. But we can talk about it tomorrow, can't we? I want to know all about how your interview comes out. You *are* staying for a couple more days, aren't you?"

Jamie nodded, though he knew they wouldn't talk about his interview. In Michael's house all you ever talked about was Michael. That, and Michael's money. Michael disappeared, followed by the sound of the front door being slammed. The slamming of the door tripped an emotional switch inside Jamie. It was a sound that resonated for him, an explosive refrain from some deep undusted recess of his mind. All at once he was a skinny nine-year-old again, and one of his father's tirades was in full show. His mother was in the kitchen, calm, but seething beneath her skin. His father was off on another planet, one that required him to torture her. In those years it happened two or three times a week until finally, a few weeks after Christmas 1963, the door-slamming stopped.

That was when his father had given up on her, because she wouldn't respond to his screaming. She had become conditioned to withdraw within herself, to let his torments go unrequited. He left one evening, closing the door quietly, and never came back.

Three

Daryl Devero leaned forward into the bay window, staring down through iron security bars to the buckled sidewalk outside his and his mother's rowhouse. He smiled as a line of ants marched anxiously for a piece of candy bar left by the man and lady who had been exercising on the front stoop the night before, prior to Daryl's mother running them off with a broom.

Daryl's smile was magical, complemented by a pair of vortexlike dimples in his round brown cheeks. He wore a silver and green Philadelphia Eagles sweat suit, and his feet were snug inside a pair of Simba the Lion King bedroom slippers. His eyes were the rich oily brown of dark roasted coffee, and they were round and sweet like a child's, although they had seen more violence and vice in four short years than most people see in a lifetime.

On this particular Tuesday morning the Deveros' block on North Fifth Street was already churning, its primary commercial venture, the drug trade, open for business to anyone who wanted a little cocaine before breakfast. The trade was centered around a group of young men down at the corner, standing outside what used to be a tavern at the end of what was once a normal working class street. The warm weather and sunshine brought out a bumper crop of customers. Young black women, thin as razors, weaved amid piles of trash on sidewalks that looked like they had been in an earthquake. Latino teenagers cruised by intermittently, the smoke black windows of their customized Toyotas open a bit to let out the blare of the stereo.

Pimple-faced white kids from the northeast suburbs prowled the block nervously, hoping to score before heading to Virginia Beach or the Jersey Shore for a spring break in the sun.

For those unafraid to get out of their cars and actually walk the block, mostly the users or prostitutes, or those who were both, North Fifth offered up an environment as hallucinogenic as anything one could get out of a pipe. Three cars, stripped bare of everything not welded to their chassis, were piled atop each other like toys outside the gates of the old shoe factory across from the Deveros' house, where the junkies liked to party. Next door to the factory were five row houses, looking as though they belonged in Sarajevo. There were black holes where doors and windows had once been, and the pock-marked brick had been wallpapered with graffiti. Just outside the De-vero's bay window, a crater the size of a small bathtub had formed in the asphalt, daring anyone to actually drive on the street. Pieces of asphalt from the hole were scattered about like chunks of ice in an ice flow.

"What, Major?"

Daryl turned back to his mother Bernice, who sat on a sofa uphol-stered in worn pale blue velour. Across the room Geraldo was holding court on a console TV. Above Bernice on the wall was a reproduction of Carracci's *Landscape with the Flight into Egypt*, a print her brother had once brought her from Rome, Italy. On top of the TV was a vase of silk flowers, into which Bernice Devero had stuck a single live daffodil, a flower she had rescued from the remains of a window box outside an abandoned house down the street.

"What?" she said again.

Daryl smiled because he knew that his mother was talking to his uncle Major, a gentle man who took care of him and his mother, al-ways helping in any way he could.

"I know," said Bernice Devero, speaking into the receiver of the phone. "But I'm telling you, Major, it's worse than ever. Last night two crack heads were doin' it right here on my front porch. Just a minute, just a minute. Baby," she looked over to Daryl, "turn that TV down for me."

Daryl waltzed across the shag carpet to the television and turned down the sound. Bernice continued her conversation.

"That's right, crackin' a nut right on my stoop. And they about stole everything, Major. At Thanksgiving, they stole a paper turkey off my door. A paper turkey!"

"Calm down, Bernice," said her brother's baritone voice. "We'll do something."

"What are we going to do?" She pushed her large square eyeglasses up on her nose. "We can't sell this house. It's worth less now than it was thirty-five years ago when Mama and Daddy bought it for eighteen thousand. And ain't that something?"

"We'll just abandon it then," said Major. "Maybe rent it out."

"Ain't nobody going rent it neither . . . except maybe for dealers or pimps. Besides, where are Daryl and I going to move? I don't have no money, except what the government give me. And for that amount, we just going to end up in another neighborhood like this one. Or worse yet, in a project."

She shifted back and let out a long sigh from her broad nose. Bernice Devero was a plump woman, and she sat in the middle of the sofa between two cushions. Her weight crushed them down, tipping the ends up like a pair of seesaws.

"I have money, Bernice," said Major. "A goodly amount. At least I will by tonight."

"You sold some paintings?" she said.

There was a pause on the line, and for a moment she thought that their long-distance connection had been cut.

"Something like that," he said. "Don't you worry about it, though. It's enough to get you and Daryl out of there. Maybe set you up in an apartment in Jersey."

Bernice smiled. The wide grin revealed a gap between her two front incisors, the only flaw to a set of brilliant white teeth.

"Get out," she said. "New Jersey?" The words rolled off her tongue as if she were speaking of Paradise itself. New Jersey was country to her, a sylvan oasis compared to the asphalt hell of North Philadelphia. She could remember the small clapboard house on a quarter acre the family had rented outside Sicklerville, back when there was farm work to be had not too far from the city. Before her father had taken a shift job at Geis Shoes, with its promise of a better life.

Her brother, two years her senior, had taken care of her back then too. Major had always been big for his age, and he was mean when he needed to be. He had kept her clear of the Irish and Polish boys who taunted her on the way to and from school. And he made sure that the young men she went out with treated her right. In fact, as Bernice now saw it, the blossoming of her and Major's relationship was the only good thing to have come about from their having moved to the city in 1955. That, and Major's discovering his artistic talent. He had found that he had a gift for drawing and painting, something he probably would never have realized away from the city. His gift had been spotted by an art teacher in the seventh grade, and it had eventually gotten him a scholarship to the Pennsylvania Academy of the Fine Arts, right after graduating Central High.

"Wherever you want to go, Bernice. Within reason."

"Thank you, Major."

Her words were tempered by the probability of disappointment. Major was a good man, and he had always helped her and Daryl. But he too often believed that he was one or two paintings away from really making it. She had seen him hurt many times, when the gallery show he was sure he was going to get didn't come through, or the surefire commission failed to materialize.

Bernice adjusted herself on the cushions and let out a long breath.

"Major?"

"Yeah?"

"You didn't do nothing bad, did you?"

Again, there was silence on the line.

"No. Just trying to make a living with my brushes."

"I don't know what kind of money you're talking about, but you never made that much off of painting. Good as you are, you always struggled."

"I've made a little now and then, Bernice. You know that. I'm not wealthy, but I'm doing all right."

Bernice stared at a caption on the TV, below one of Geraldo's guests. A young white woman with blond hair as big as Texas was smiling. The superimposed caption read *Slept with Over 150 Rock Stars in 1996.*

"Thank you, Major. I love you."

"I love you too, baby. Kiss the boy for me. Bye now."

Bernice hung up the phone slowly, savoring the call like a teenage girl hanging up from a conversation with a boyfriend. She then worked her way out of the sinkhole in the sofa, and walked over to the bay window. Daryl was still staring out at North Fifth in silent wonder. Bernice reached up and quietly pulled across a sheer curtain, blocking out his view. She was always doing that, it seemed, blocking out his view. She sat next to him on the window seat and wrapped him up in her arms. He looked up at her and smiled his infectious smile, and she kissed him on the forehead. She then gazed across the room to the print above the sofa.

Jesus and Mary, she thought in her silent short form prayer, let him get the money this time, please Lord, let him get it.

Ramsgill and Elena took a cab across town, and just before one o'-clock, Elena headed to work at Marilyn Foster Gallery while Ramsgill made his way to Laycutt/Farr Architects.

The Rittenhouse Square offices of Laycutt/Farr looked like an odd hybrid between a Giorgio de Chirico painting and an Antarctic landscape. The offices were housed in a two-story loft that ran straight through from Walnut Street to an alley behind. The space was two hundred feet deep and only thirty feet wide, with walls of glass situated front and back, a mezzanine to one side. The color scheme was white on white on white again, a modernist's wet dream. Two towers stood like miniature buildings in the central space, set at third points along the way. The towers were cool, unadorned planes of white, punctuated with smooth arches below and small square windows above. The walls of the towers were battered, as were the side walls of the space itself. The planes shifted and overlapped, jutting up into the space like fingers of ice, their tops forming irregular crenellations, concealing lights that bathed the ceiling in a warm glow.

Ramsgill was shown up a spiral stair to the top of one of the towers, within which was a small conference room. A few moments later a slender man with jet black hair and rectangular wire-rim glasses appeared. He wore a wool blazer and khaki pants, along with a bright red tie. He had the kind, intelligent face of a surgeon, but it was a face awash with anxiety.

"Jamie?"

Ramsgill rose and reached out his hand to Tod Farr. Farr held a legal pad with a pen clipped to it, which slapped when he dropped it to the table.

"How about coffee?" Farr said, shaking Ramsgill's hand.

"No thanks," said Ramsgill.

Farr sat, as did Ramsgill.

"Is something the matter?" Ramsgill asked.

Farr nodded, his pale yellow eyes like a pair of full moons rising over a dark horizon. "I'm afraid we're not going to have your interview today, Jamie. I had my secretary try to reach you in Princeton, but I guess you'd already left."

"I've been down since yesterday," said Ramsgill. "Staying with my brother."

Farr nodded again.

"What's up?" Ramsgill said.

"How long have you known David?" said Farr. He leaned forward, placing his hands on the table before him. He nervously played his thumbs against the backs of his hands.

"Since we were at Penn together," said Ramsgill. "I met him freshman year, though he was third year at the time. We shared a house on Spruce Street for a semester."

"And you're pretty good friends?"

"Pretty good, I suppose. I don't have to tell you, Tod, that David doesn't really have friends. He's married to this place, you know that. He comes up to the architecture school as a guest critic now and then, and we have lunch when he's in Princeton for work. Why? What's the matter?"

"I don't know how to say this, Jamie. And I'd sure as hell appreciate it if you'd keep it quiet. But David came into work today like always. He had a full plate like always. Several people were waiting to see him when he excused himself to go to the bathroom but never came back. He must have left the office by the back stair. He's AWOL."

"He didn't tell anybody where he was going?"

"No."

"And you haven't heard from him?"

"Nope."

Ramsgill shrugged. He looked across the loft and out one of the large windows. The steel frame of Keystone Place stood out in the midday sun.

"Well, maybe the pressure of work is getting to him," he said.

Farr belted out a laugh, a long full laugh, but one that ended up hollow. He shook his head.

"Not a chance, Jamie. David's a *charette* animal. He thrives on pressure. He's busted his ass for two months on our design for the *Lindenstrasse* Competition. Those drawings are going to be air-shipped to Europe tonight. There's no way he would have left that hanging. I mean there is a way, because he obviously did it, but not because of pressure."

"So what gives?"

"Do you have any idea if David knows anyone in Jim Thorpe, Jamie?"

"Jim Thorpe? The old coal town upstate?"

Farr nodded.

"No. I mean I probably wouldn't anyway. Why?"

Farr lifted up the first sheet of his legal pad and slipped out a long rectangular piece of paper which rested beneath it. He handed it to Ramsgill. It was an ivory business envelope of laid linen stock with one end ripped open. It was addressed to David Laycutt in care of Laycutt/Farr Architects and it had been posted by a single first-class stamp two days before. There was a return address of 41 Packer Avenue, Jim Thorpe, PA. The postmark also bore Jim Thorpe as the post office of origin. The sender's name was not given in the return address.

"What do you make of it?" said Farr.

Ramsgill tilted the letter into the light.

"I don't know," said Ramsgill. "Letter from a friend? It doesn't look like a business letter because there's no salutation. It's addressed to David Laycutt, no Mr. But what does this have to do with David's disappearing?"

"He got the letter this morning. He had just gotten into the office, had four people dying to see him, and while he was talking on his office phone, he picked the letter up out of a stack on his desk. One of the kids said that when he picked it up he literally turned white. The idiot hung up on a new client, stuffed the envelope into his pocket, and bolted for the bathroom. That was the last anybody saw of him. The envelope was found later on the floor outside the bathroom. He must have taken the letter with him."

Ramsgill started to hand the envelope back to Farr, then paused.

"Did you try to contact this . . . a person at this address?" he said.

"How?"

"Call the police. Find out who lives there."

Farr sat back, his hands still fidgeting before him. "You sure you don't want coffee?"

Ramsgill shook his head. He watched as Farr's eyes traveled the conference room before settling back on him.

"I don't want the police involved, Jamie."

"Afraid of the publicity?"

"Partly. But it's bigger than that."

"What?"

Farr looked up from his hands and stared into Ramsgill's clear blue eyes.

"Jamie, I'm going to tell you this because you're David's friend. And because I'm at wit's end. But so help me, you've got to be quiet about it."

"What?"

"After David left here this morning our bookkeeper called in payroll. About an hour later she gets a call back from the payroll service, saying that there's not enough in the accounts to cover today's checks. So she phones our bank, and they tell her that David came in there this morning, not long after leaving here. He withdrew seventy-five thousand dollars."

"Oh shit," said Ramsgill.

"Oh shit is right. We're not talking pocket change here."

The muffled sound of the air conditioner kicking on came from the trusses above them, and Ramsgill could feel a slightly cool, but faint, jet of air.

"Seventy-five thousand dollars? What's David need that kind of money for?"

"I don't know," said Farr. "But suddenly the whole office is abuzz, and I had to call a staff meeting to calm everybody down. Not only that, but to warn them that anybody that lets this get out of the office will get their butt canned. Do you know what would happen if this got out? Other firms in town would use it against us. Rumors would have us out of business faster than a Michael Johnson four-forty. You know how competitive the architectural community is."

"There's got to be a logical explanation, Tod."

Farr was staring down at his hands again, his head motionless, his body as stiff as a cadaver.

"You'd think so," he said. "But I'm not sure. Technically, David can take money out of the account because he's a partner. I'm worried he won't come back. Then what? Do I try to help him because he's in trouble and has been my partner for twenty years? Or prosecute him because he's run off with the firm's money?"

"You help him, don't you? At least give him the benefit of the doubt."

"I suppose."

A phone on the table buzzed and Farr jerked it up.

He listened for a moment, then said, "I can't talk to Connelly right now, Rita. I don't care how important he says it is. And tell Sir Anthony I'll call him in an hour. What? Yeah, I guess it is evening already over there. All right. I'll *try* to call in fifteen minutes. Tell him I'm sorry."

Farr hung up without saying another word.

"I don't know how I'm going to deal with this, Jamie. Besides taking David's workload I've got to find the big goofball. Serves me right for shacking up in business with a mad artist."

"I could help," said Ramsgill.

Farr's body didn't move but his eyes flicked in Ramsgill's direction.

"No. This is my problem. And I'm sorry this had to happen to you. David had me convinced to bring you onboard. But I can't focus on that right now."

"I understand," Ramsgill said. "But I mean it, I do want to help."

"It's nothing you want to get mixed up—"

"Tod, it *is* something I want to get mixed up in. Look at it this way: I want a job. Without David around, and until you're capable of putting the office back together, I'm doing nothing but sitting on my hands."

"There are other places to interview. Sane places."

"I know that."

Ramsgill stared at him for a good five seconds then Farr said, "Suit yourself, Jamie. What do you want to do?"

Ramsgill pondered for a moment, his eagerness to help far ahead of any logical plan.

"I'll look for him," he said. "Go to his apartment, to Jim Thorpe, whatever."

"You can look at the apartment," Farr said. "But Ann's already been by there."

"Ann?"

"David's secretary. She went by earlier."

"No sign of him?"

"No. "

"I'll check anyway," said Ramsgill. "Then head upstate."

"If you go to Jim Thorpe, you might as well stop by David's mountain house. It's where he spends his free time, what little he has of it.

We called there, but got no answer. I can get you the keys."

"Good," said Ramsgill. "Now what about his apartment? Is he still living at the Dorchester?"

"Yes."

"I'll need a car."

"Take mine," said Farr. "It's in the garage behind the office."

"Okay. By the way, what's David driving?"

"An Acura. Dark green."

Ramsgill filed the information away in his head.

"What else?" said Farr, glancing down at his watch.

"I know you have to make your phone calls," said Ramsgill. "But a couple of more minutes?"

"Sure."

"Tell me truthfully," said Ramsgill. "How's the financial health of the firm?"

"Truthfully? It's never been better."

"And David's financial situation?"

Farr tilted his head to one side. He pushed out his lips, making a puckering gesture.

"I don't know what he does with his money, Jamie, but he makes plenty. *Plenty.* I'm happy for that, at least."

"What do you mean?"

"It hasn't always been easy for him. You must remember that from when you were in school. Small-town guy. His dad was a coal miner. My significant other's an investment banker. And I had money from my grandfather when we started this business. But David's always struggled. Until recently, that is."

"How about David's personal life, Tod?"

"He has no family left, you know that, Jamie. An only child. No wife to run around on, no kids to worry about. Lives like a monk. He'll see one or two socialites on occasion, but that's more for convenience than anything else. An escort to go to openings and galas with, nothing serious. The people he's closest to are our clients, I suppose. He spends an inordinate amount of time with them. Entertaining them, keeping them happy."

"Do you have a list of clients?"

"I could have one made up. Or, I . . . wait a minute."

Farr picked up the phone.

"Rita, could you bring a job list up to the conference room? Thanks."

As Farr hung up, Ramsgill was once again fingering the envelope.

"Tell me," said Ramsgill. "Let's say we agree that David's not close to anyone, that he's married to his work, and that the firm is in good financial shape. Let's even assume that he is in good financial shape."

"Okay."

"He gets a letter which is presumably from an individual. There's no salutation, it's not certified, it's not from a bank or a lawyer or a collection agency. At least from the return address it doesn't appear to be."

"All right."

"And let's remember that it was the letter that made him flee. Not a phone call from a hospital or from the police. No relative in trouble, no authorities after him."

"Fine."

"So what kind of letter was it? And don't forget the seventy-five thousand."

"Blackmail?"

"Has to be. What else would make a middle-aged man in the prime of his professional life disappear, taking a large amount of his firm's money with him?"

"But why?"

"You tell me."

Farr shrugged, forming V-like lines on his brow.

"And who . . . ?"

A middle-aged woman with teased brown hair and a crooked grin appeared at the top of the spiral stair.

"Here's the list," she said. She disappeared as quickly as she had come.

Farr glanced at the list for a moment before passing it Ramsgill's way. Ramsgill took it and immediately began to scrutinize it. The jobs were listed by year, in reverse chronological order. A few names stood out, recognizable from Philadelphia society or business, and in more recent years, international institutions.

"I just thought of something," he said, putting down the list.

"What?"

"If this is blackmail, then don't you think it odd that the blackmailer would have used a letter to contact David?"

"Why?"

"Because a letter leaves physical evidence. I mean, why not just telephone him?"

"Maybe the blackmailer doesn't know him."

"Can't be. Remember what your employee said. He said that David turned white when he saw the envelope. That means the address meant something to him."

"I guess you're right."

"Also, David took off like a bat out of hell. He withdrew money which, if we're right, is payoff money. That means that the letter must have designated a date and time for a meeting with David. But what if the letter had been delayed? Or what if the letter was delivered a few days early? Then David might have mulled things over, and have decided to go to the police. If I were a blackmailer I would make my demand outright, and give David a very short time in which to respond. That would have accounted for his having dropped everything and gone to the bank immediately."

"I suppose."

Ramsgill sat back, thinking about Laycutt, the situation, and how it didn't hold together. As an architect Ramsgill was used to parts relating to the whole. He didn't like inconsistencies, things that didn't fit patterns.

"Jamie?" Farr again looked at his watch.

"I know," said Ramsgill.

"Sorry."

"Just get me the keys."

They both rose, and Farr followed Ramsgill to the top of the spiral stair.

"By the way," said Ramsgill, looking over a half-height wall down to the studio space below. "What do you want me to do if I find him?"

Farr thought for a moment, then spoke.

"Have him telephone me. I just want to talk."

"And the money?"

"If he still has it, I want it back."

Ramsgill nodded.

"And if he doesn't have it?" said Ramsgill.

"Then that's between him and me."

Four

David Laycutt turned into the gravel parking area and pulled his car up to a long gray metal building whose panels were rusting at their joints. As he shut the car door, he thought once more about what he was doing here, about the consequences of it all. For the entire drive up from Philly his mind had played games of denial, then once reality sank in, it circumvented his options, weighing the probable outcome of each.

The right thing to do, of course, would have been to go to the police. Blackmail was against the law, and the police would know what to do about it. But they would also ask questions and things would come out. It wouldn't be long before the layers of deceit were peeled away to reveal the truth he had managed to keep secret for decades. And then his run would be over. The years of hard work, the sleepless nights, the times without money—all to achieve a stature he had never dreamed of in his profession—would have been for naught.

Then what about the other options? He could pay the blackmail money and take his chances, but that too would ruin him. Even if his blackmailer stayed quiet Laycutt would have to answer to Tod Farr about what he had done with the seventy-five thousand. And if Tod could see to forgive him, or even forget the debt, it would still put the firm in difficult straits, and it would be another couple of years before they could balance the books. Enough time to elapse for the blackmailer to think about it again, to perhaps send another letter.

Then there was the third possibility. Confront his blackmailer.

Threaten him. Tell him you'll take him down with you. See if he falls for the bluff. Doubtful, though. He doesn't have half as much to lose as you do, Laycutt. And besides, you can't afford to go down.

Which left one option.

Kill him.

Laycutt paused for a moment and took a deep breath, the brisk upstate air drilling into his lungs. He then started forward. The end of the building had a huge roll-up door for moving stone in and out, and beside it, to the left, a human door, which looked about as insignificant as Laycutt felt. He opened that door by sliding a wooden bar to one side, then stepped in.

Beyond was a dusty world, encapsulated by a din of mechanical noise. The place smelled of oil and of an acrid odor that was slightly metallic. Huge machines—grinders, wet saws, turntables, conveyors, hoist ways—cluttered the space. From above, light tried to force its way through filthy clearstory windows, filling the space with only the dimmest glow. Slabs of slate stood everywhere around him, piled up on the dirt floor that really wasn't dirt at all but rather charcoal gray slate dust. There were wall caps, paving blocks, cornices, tombstones—pieces of every shape and description, all the same monotonous gray, which in the cave-like space appeared black. In the distance an old man could be seen, tipping one of the slabs up onto a two-wheeled cart. His body was a dirty, rumpled mess, and for a moment Laycutt could see him as a vision of his own father, crawling wearily out of a narrow mine shaft at the end of a day.

Laycutt was about to go over to the man and inquire about Paskiewicz when out of the shadows appeared a face—all smudge and sweat—looking much older than he had remembered it.

"Dave?" said the voice that accompanied the face.

David Laycutt paused, thinking again of his options, if he really wanted to go through with this. He shook Ray Paskiewicz's hand.

"How are you, Ray?"

Paskiewicz took a pink rag from the pocket of his work suit and wiped a forehead that was as dirty as the inside of a chimney flue. He was a small man with a cleft chin and protruding brown eyes. He had always reminded Laycutt of Michael J. Pollard, the actor who had played the impish cohort of Bonnie and Clyde in Arthur Penn's film.

"I'm all right," he said. "Not a famous architect like my old running buddy, but I can't complain."

"That's good. And how's Yvonne and the kids?"

"Yvette," Paskiewicz corrected. "And they're fine."

"Look, I'm a little nervous, Ray. Do you mind if we . . . ?"

"Yeah, let's go outside."

Paskiewicz walked over to a machine that looked like a giant turntable made of sheet steel, perhaps ten feet in diameter. A lanky man was shoveling sand up onto its surface, and two other men stood over the turntable, watching slabs of stone float on the wet drum. Paskiewicz motioned to one of the men with his thumb, an indication that he was taking a break.

"What's that thing do?" said Laycutt, as they walked toward the door.

"Takes the slabs down to thickness. Float a stone on it and it'll take a half inch off in ten minutes. You can imagine what it would do to your rear end if you got it caught on there. Would outdo lyposuction, that's for sure."

Paskiewicz blurted a laugh, then opened the door, squinting as his eyes met the sunlight. Laycutt walked through. Outside again, Laycutt looked around him. The gravel parking lot was the same insidious gray as the plant floor. Surrounding the parking area on all sides were mounds of slate, some thirty or forty feet high. They looked like God's own trash dump, dull gray heaps of stone, dusted in some crevices with the vestiges of winter snow.

"My truck's over here," said Paskiewicz.

Laycutt followed, noticing that Paskiewicz walked with a limp that he hadn't had when they were kids. Paskiewicz's truck was an old blue Dodge, parked at the edge of the parking area. When they reached it, Paskiewicz stuck his hand through the open window on the driver's side, and opened the door from within. The door groaned in protest. The odor of stale cigarettes drifted out of the cab.

"To say I was surprised to hear from you would be a hell of an understatement."

"Yeah, I suppose," said Laycutt. "I never get up here any more now that my folks are dead."

"Oh, really?" said Paskiewicz. "Bob Parkins told me you had a cabin over in Birch Run."

Laycutt started to hem and haw and Paskiewicz felt embarrassed for him, so he spoke again.

"Do you know what you're doing, Dave?" Paskiewicz slid onto the seat and looked over to Laycutt.

"If I knew what I was doing, Ray, I wouldn't have called."

"What are you going to use it for?"

"I'm not going to use it, at least I don't think so. I have some business with a man I used to know. I'm going to try to convince him to stop harassing me."

Paskiewicz paused for a moment, weighing Laycutt's statement. He then reached under the passenger-side seat and pulled out a crumpled paper bag. He slipped out a semiautomatic pistol, and Laycutt thought of how ridiculous a gun looked slipping out of a paper bag, as if it were a grocery item. No less ridiculous, he realized, than the notion of his actually using the gun.

"Guns don't convince people," Paskiewicz said. "You can threaten with a gun, and you might get the answer you want to hear, but if you don't use it, you'll be right back where you started. And if you do use it, then, well, you're screwed. I'm an expert at that. Four years in Graterford."

Laycutt thought about that, and about how he had already made up his mind to use the gun. What Paskiewicz didn't realize was that he was screwed whether he used it or not. He took the pistol and rested it in the palm of his hand. It was heavier than he had imagined, especially for such a small thing.

"How much do I owe you?" said Laycutt.

"Well, the fellow I got it from wanted three hundred dollars, but he was trying to fuck me over. It's a Raven, for chrissake. I gave him a hundred and that's what I'll sell it to you for, Dave. But you got to promise me something. You don't know where you got it. My parole officer would . . . well, you know what I mean."

Laycutt looked up to his old friend.

"Promise, Ray. And you've got to promise me too. You don't know who you gave it to."

Laycutt then pulled some bills from his pocket. They were new and he had a hard time separating them. When he had gotten some of them apart he gave them to Paskiewicz. Paskiewicz slid out of the truck and shut the door with a *clang*.

"Don't use it, Davey."

Laycutt nodded, but he really wasn't paying attention. "This place hasn't changed much," he said, looking around him, remembering when, as kids, they used to climb the slate heaps, always aware that avalanches were imminent. He recalled that Paskiewicz was the most daring, unfazed by danger.

"Wind Gap never changes, Dave, you know that. You're just lucky you got out."

"So look, tell your family hello," Laycutt said. "And thanks for this."

"Don't worry about it."

Laycutt grasped Paskiewicz's shoulder, taking the money he had given his friend out of his hand. He folded it over and pushed it into the pocket of Paskiewicz's work shirt. He then looked into Paskiewicz's eyes and clutched his shoulder again before turning and walking away. As he crossed the parking area, he considered Paskiewicz's words. He didn't feel lucky to have gotten out of Wind Gap—not at the moment, not in the least.

The Dorchester was a post-war building whose geometric concrete and glass exterior held about as much charm as a television set. It was clear to Ramsgill, however, that the tower's residents didn't live there because of its charm, but rather because it fronted Rittenhouse Square and had panoramic views of the city. He showed the apartment key to the concierge, saying that he worked for Laycutt, and that he was picking something up for him.

Laycutt's apartment was on the twenty-fifth floor, a two-level corner unit facing the square. It was nicely furnished, but hardly extravagant. The living and dining areas were open to one another, wrapping a small kitchen. The kitchen was outfitted in simple overlay cabinets, and yet they were painted an unusual mustard yellow, which imbued them with a quality of richness. The cabinet-door handles were green wooden Roman numerals, each one a different number, which made for a most unusual effect. Lined up above the cabinets was a collection of simple yet elegant metal cookie tins from the early part of the century. The refrigerator was vintage Philco, circa 1955.

A baby grand piano anchored one end of the living room, and an enormous couch covered in white muslin held down the other. Over the sofa hung a reproduction of Nolli's famous 1747 map of Rome. The sofa was flanked by two Mies van der Rohe Barcelona chairs, expensive, yet Ramsgill had known many an architect to plunk down their last three thousand dollars to own the coveted seating. The rest of the furniture was eclectic, contemporary mixed with odd pieces from different periods, the kind of antiques whose aesthetic value weigh their rarity.

In the kitchen Ramsgill found a notepad next to the phone which held a collection of scribbled messages. They were mostly phone numbers for local establishments: a few restaurants, a dry cleaner, a health club. There was one long page of notes from a conversation with a travel agent, regarding what looked to be a planned summer trip to the Veneto. None of them appeared to be related to Laycutt's disappearance. The refrigerator and cabinets held nothing of interest either, other than the fact that Laycutt seemed to have a penchant for Indian food and Belgian beer. The refrigerator was definitely that of a bachelor, Spartan, and filled mostly with condiments that had been in there so long that their labels were wilting.

Ramsgill made his way to the second floor, climbing a stair constructed of diamond-plate steel treads and suspended by aircraft cable. In the master bedroom and bath he came up empty, but in a second bedroom which Laycutt apparently used as a study, he found the first signs of Laycutt's presence in the apartment after having left the office. In the middle of the study was an oval glass-topped desk, and on the desk were a number of items. Amidst the clutter was a withdrawal slip from Mellon Bank, in the amount of $75,000.

Also on the desk was a gray leather day-timer turned to today's date. Written in at the top of the page were the words FARBER BENSALEM and a phone number. The name was familiar but Ramsgill couldn't remember from where. He decided to try the number. He picked up the phone and started to dial, but then paused, wondering who else Laycutt might have called. The blackmail letter had come from Jim Thorpe, and Ramsgill knew that Bensalem was a suburb of Philadelphia, north on the Delaware River, nowhere near Jim Thorpe. Would Laycutt have tried to contact his blackmailer? To plead with him? To bargain? Instead of calling the number in Bensalem, Ramsgill hit the redial button on the phone.

He brought the receiver up to his ear and waited patiently as the phone rang once, and then again. On the sixth ring, an answering machine clicked on. Ramsgill listened, and jotted down the message. But it wasn't from anyone named Farber. It was a deep voice, possibly that of a black man. He transcribed hastily, "You've reached Major Devereaux. I'm not in at the moment, but if you'd please leave your name and number, I'll get back to you as soon as I can." The machine beeped, and for a brief second, Ramsgill considered leaving a message. Instead he hung up.

He sat staring at the name he had written in the date book. He underlined *Major Devereaux,* then stared at it some more. This Devereaux guy was the last person Laycutt had spoken with.

He then dialed the number in Bensalem.

"Dr. Farber's residence," a female voice answered in a thick accent.

"Yes, my name is Ramsgill. Is . . . Dr. Farber in?"

"You're Cate Chew's husband?"

"No. Actually, my brother is. . . . "

Ramsgill suddenly realized that this was the Dr. Farber who owned the Eakins painting.

"Mr. Ramsgill?"

"I'm sorry. What?"

"Was there something I could help you with? I'm Vibeke Lidz, Dr. Farber's secretary."

"Oh," Ramsgill stammered. "Yes, I'm trying to locate David Laycutt. I thought he might have phoned there today."

Now, the woman herself paused.

"Actually he did."

"What time was that?"

"This morning."

"Did he speak to Dr. Farber?"

"No. The doctor's at the hospital all day."

"Which hospital would that be?"

"Pennsylvania."

"I see. But you say that David did call?"

"I did."

"Did he seem upset? I'm a little worried about him."

"He seemed like he was in a hurry. I told him that Dr. Farber was in surgery at the hospital, and that he'd be there until later on this afternoon. I also told him that if it were really urgent he could leave Dr. Farber a message on his beeper. That didn't seem to be what he wanted to hear."

"What do you mean?"

"He just said that he had to speak with him right away. That it couldn't wait."

"Did he say what it was about?"

"I'm afraid I couldn't tell you if he had, Mr. Ramsgill. But no, he gave me no indication why he was calling."

"Okay. Well look, I'd like to speak with Dr. Farber myself. Please tell him I phoned. I'm going to be on the road so it doesn't make sense to leave a number. I'll try him again later."

He thanked her and hung up.

He immediately dialed Cate at the museum. While he was put on hold, he considered the coincidence of David Laycutt's knowing Dr. Farber. And the coincidence of his being anxious to speak with Farber that morning, of all mornings.

"Cate? Hi, it's Jamie."

"Jamie, where are you?"

"I'm at David Laycutt's apartment. Listen—"

"Slow down. How'd your interview go?"

"I didn't have it."

"No?"

"No. It seems that David has left town unannounced and I'm not going to have the interview until he gets back. But what I wanted to ask you was, did you know that David knew Dr. Farber, the man who owns the Eakins painting?"

"I don't think so. But then that doesn't surprise me. They're both heavyweights in the arts community, Farber as a benefactor, Laycutt as doyen. I'm sure their paths have crossed."

"I keep thinking about the Eakins painting. How it was a fake, then it wasn't a fake, how Farber got his hands on it . . . "

"What does this have to do with David Laycutt, Jamie?"

Ramsgill wanted to tell her that Laycutt had phoned Farber that morning, just after withdrawing the money from the bank. In Laycutt's state of mind it wouldn't have been a social call. Farber had to have something to do with his disappearance. But Ramsgill realized that he owed it to Tod Farr not to tell Cate the truth.

"I don't know that it actually does have anything to do with David. Do you know a man named Major Devereaux?" he asked instead.

She hesitated.

"Devereaux? No, not that I recall. Why?"

"Oh nothing."

"Listen, Jamie, if we're going to play twenty questions I get my turn. I don't know what you're driving at, but I don't like the sound of it. Why do you want to know all this?"

"Sorry, Cate, but I can't tell you. Look, I'd better run. And about dinner tonight . . . "

"Michael phoned Jamie and apologized. He said he still can't make it for dinner, but he realizes he's been a jerk. He's been under a lot of pressure at work."

"Yeah, sure."

"And, Jamie, he also told me something I never thought I'd hear him say."

"What?"

"He's sorry about your father. And about what he did."

Ramsgill looked across Laycutt's study, the empty feeling inside returning. The memory of his father's death chafed at him, and he was unable to make it subside.

"He told you that, huh?"

"Yes."

"Then why doesn't he tell me?"

"You know better than I do that he's not good at expressing feelings, Jamie. He and I can have a fight, and afterward, even after I apologize, he just turns inward and doesn't say anything. But he changes. For the next two or three days he'll treat me like royalty, and I realize that's his way of saying he's sorry."

"We're not talking about a fight, Cate. We're talking about the fact that he admitted Dad to the hospital with inoperable lymphoma, and never bothered to tell me to come home."

"He did tell you to come home, Jamie."

"For God's sake, he told me after Dad had died."

"He didn't know what was going to happen, Jamie. He thought your dad would only be in for a day or two. And you were in Italy. What was he going to do? Have you fly home to find out that your dad had been released already? He didn't want you to worry."

Ramsgill clenched his jaw and fought back emotion.

"And because he's my big brother, he knew what was right for me. Don't you think I should have had a say in it?"

"Yes, you probably should."

"I never even got to see Dad before he died."

Cate let out a long, slow breath.

"I'm sorry, Jamie."

Ramsgill paused, realizing he had no right to take this out on his sister-in-law. It was just the pent-up frustration, compounded by the fact that he had never had the nerve to confront Michael about it himself.

"I am too," he said.

"So you and Elena and I will go out tonight," said Cate.

"I don't think so," Ramsgill said.

"Why?"

"I've got to do something. I probably won't be back until later on tonight."

"Back from where?"

Ramsgill's thoughts were still half with his father, trying to shove what Cate had told him into the memory box that occupied a corner of his mind's attic.

"I can't tell you," he said reluctantly. "But look, I'll call you later on and tell you for sure if I can't make it."

"And Elena? Do you want me to pass along the message? Or are you going to phone her?"

Ramsgill looked at his watch. It was almost three-thirty, and he realized he had to get on the road.

"If you talk to her, tell her I'll phone her in a little while."

"Okay. Is that it?"

"I guess. Oh, one more thing. What was the name of Mrs. Addison's niece? The one who runs her shop now?"

"Anne Holden. Why?"

"Do you have her number?"

Ramsgill waited a moment, before Cate gave it to him.

"Jamie, I don't know what you're up to, but I really don't like the sound of it."

"I'm up to nothing. And look, I'll see you guys shortly."

"Bye then."

"Talk to you later."

Ramsgill hung up, then stood and walked over to an étagère on Laycutt's study wall. He had been staring at a photograph on one of the glass shelves. The photograph was of three men. A much younger Laycutt stood to the left of a man in Ben Franklin glasses, from whom he seemed to be accepting a certificate of some kind. Laycutt was taller than the man, with a large head and a straight wide mouth, sporting a Fu Manchu mustache. The man next to him might have been in his forties, distinguished looking, with a sharp face that bordered on gauntness. To the second man's right was a black gentleman of slender build, who was already holding a certificate. He had a paper-thin mustache and very dark skin, and a bold mouth. He and Laycutt wore blazers and wide neckties, while the other man wore a light brown suit. The picture was posed in what looked to be a ballroom, and the fill light on their faces affirmed the presence of a professional photographer. Behind them were tables topped by white tablecloths, and each table held a centerpiece of flowers. Ramsgill guessed the picture to be from an awards dinner of some sort, but from their dress, from Laycutt's full head of hair and his dated mustache, the ceremony had taken place many years before. Ramsgill guessed the 1970s.

He walked back over to the desk and, on a credenza behind it, he found a Philadelphia telephone directory. He thumbed through the D's until he came to the name *Devereaux*. There were nine listings, but none for a person named Major. He began calling them all, reaching someone at six of the numbers. None of the people he spoke to had ever heard of a Major Devereaux. One of the numbers was busy, one rang a dozen times without an answer, and one was answered by a machine. He jotted down these three numbers, determined to try them again later. Just as he was about to close the book he considered another possibility—that of other spellings. His eyes followed his finger down the page, past Deveren, Devernt, Deverenz. They settled on Devero. Four listings. On the second try, he got someone.

"Is Major Devero in, please?"

There was noise in the background that sounded like a racing car engine, and a tiny voice calling, "Mama."

"Major?" said a woman, definitely an African-American. "Major don't live here. Not no more."

Ramsgill paused and considered how to get what he needed to know out of the woman. He figured he had one shot at it, and he didn't want to waste it.

"Is this Mrs. Devero?" he asked cautiously.

The woman coughed, and it seemed as if she were laughing. Again there was a pause.

"Sorry," the woman said. "That's just funny, that's all. No, this is Bernice. I'm Major's sister."

"But you say Major doesn't live there anymore?"

"No. He got out thirty years ago."

"Where does he live now?"

"Who is this?"

Her voice had edged on a dime, turning from cooperative to suspicious. It was a throaty voice, and she seemed to struggle through her breathing.

"My name's Jamie Ramsgill. I'm looking for a friend of mine, David Laycutt. I believe he knows your brother."

"Well, if he knows my brother, then he knows he lives upstate."

"Where?" Ramsgill felt a tinge of adrenaline, as if he were coming into possession of some secret knowledge, something fleeting, something dangerous.

"I don't think I should be telling you that," she said.

"Jim Thorpe?"

There was a pregnant silence and Ramsgill realized he had hit. In the background he could hear more commotion, and the tiny voice again calling for its mother.

"I gotta go," Bernice Devero said.

"But—"

Ramsgill ended up talking to a dial tone.

He scribbled down Bernice Devero's number and address, and along with Farber's, stuffed them into his pocket. He then telephoned directory assistance for Jim Thorpe and asked for the number of Major Devero. He was told by the operator that the number was unlisted, so he called the Jim Thorpe Post Office. He reached a clerk.

"I have an address on Packer Avenue," he said. "I'd like to confirm that a certain person lives there. Forty-one Packer. The person's name is Devero."

"Is this a residence?" said the clerk.

"I suppose."

"Well, if it's a residence, we don't give out that information."

"But . . . "

"Sorry, those are the rules."

"What if it were business instead?"

"Then I could . . . wait a minute. Did you say *Packer* Avenue?"

"Yes."

"Well there's only four addresses on Packer Avenue anyway, including the Packer Mansion. And I can tell you, each one of them gets their mail here at the Post Office. In a box."

Ramsgill wondered what the clerk meant.

"I don't understand," he said. "Why is that?"

"Where are you calling from?"

"Philadelphia."

"Figures," said the clerk. "Guess you don't know Jim Thorpe. If you could see Packer Avenue, you'd know what I mean. It's too steep to deliver mail on in the winter. We don't go up there."

"Oh, I see," said Ramsgill. "All right, thanks for your time."

He hung up, no closer to knowing if the address on Packer Avenue belonged to Major Devero. But the coincidence of Devero's living in Jim Thorpe, and the fact that Laycutt's letter had come from there, was too great to ignore. He would have plenty of time to mull it over on his drive north. He rose from Laycutt's desk and made his way out the door.

Five

Ramsgill left the city at four fifteen, heading northwest on I-76. The expressway followed the sinuous course of the Schuylkill River, and like the river, it was a slow moving stream. The heavy traffic wound through Fairmount Park, eight thousand acres of promenades, ball fields, bicycle paths, gardens, and urban wilderness. He passed the Art Museum and the neoclassical Fairmount Waterworks, then the boathouses laid out along the water like a long shelf full of Victorian hats. The rowing clubs were out in force, their shells filling the imaginary lanes of the wide watercourse, just as the traffic filled six lanes of highway. The scene was illuminated in oblique orange light, the same warm light Thomas Eakins had captured so perfectly in his famous rowing pictures a century before.

Reaching the city limits, the valley in which both the river and highway were situated steepened, and the river traversed a succession of falls. At Conshohocken, he took the Blue Route north to the Pennsylvania Turnpike, and in a matter of minutes he was on the Northeast Extension, heading toward Allentown and the Poconos beyond.

As he settled into the drive, he used Tod Farr's car phone to call Farr.

"Jamie, what's up?"

"I'm heading to the Poconos."

"Anything new?"

Ramsgill explained that he had been to Laycutt's apartment, and that Laycutt had been there before him.

"He placed two calls that I know about," said Ramsgill. "One to a doctor named Harold Farber. And one to a man named Major Devero."

"Farber and Devero? Whoa, those are names from the past."

"You know them?"

"Sure," said Farr. "Though I haven't seen Devero in years. Boy, he must have jumped right off the planet."

"Actually he jumped to Jim Thorpe."

"He lives in Jim Thorpe?"

"Yeah."

"So the letter was from him?"

"It appears that way. But tell me, how does David know them?"

"In the early seventies Farber set up a fellowship program in the arts. He's a big benefactor. I'm not sure, but I think Devero and David received fellowships the same year. In fact, it might have been the program's inaugural year."

"Do you remember *what* year?"

"Oh, seventy-three or seventy-four. I know that it was before David and I started our business. The two of us were still working for Lane McCleary's firm at the time."

"I see. What do you know about Devero? Is he an architect?"

"No. He's an artist, a damn good painter, but he never really lived up to his potential. It surprises me, though, that he lives upstate. I didn't know he'd dropped out so completely."

"How about Farber?"

"Farber's a very rich man. You know that neck collar people wear for whiplash or broken necks? Farber invented it. He made a fortune before he was forty."

"And he's an art collector, right?"

"Art collector, house collector, wife collector. The current Mrs. Farber is probably thirty. Farber must be sixty-five."

"What kind of art does he collect?"

"Everything. Contemporary, Americana, sculpture."

"Did you know he owns a Thomas Eakins?"

"No. The only person I've ever known who owned an Eakins was Ellie Addison."

"What'd you say?"

"Elinor Addison. The antiques dealer. When we were working for her she came into an incredible Eakins painting."

"You worked for her?"

"Sure, Jamie. Didn't you go through the rest of that job list?"

Ramsgill had intended to go through the list on the drive up to the Poconos. It was on the seat next to him.

"No," he said.

"Yes, Mrs. Addison and her husband, God, what was his name . . . oh, Brook . . . Jamie, they were our very first client."

Ramsgill turned to the back of the job list and could see that for 1976 Laycutt/Farr had only three clients. The first of the three was Brook and Elinor Addison.

"David knew Mr. Addison through some family connection," said Farr. "But I guess he never figured he'd get into that morass."

"What morass?"

"Well, the job was a renovation of the Addison's house out in Bryn Mawr. A beautiful eighteenth-century farmhouse with outbuildings and so on. And it was David's job. But he lowballed the fee because we needed the work, and then Brook Addison died midway through the project and Mrs. Addison took over. She liked to have driven David crazy."

"What do you mean?"

"She changed her mind incessantly, couldn't make decisions on time, had the builder deviate from our plans. She drank a lot and her mind was like a sieve. David got sucked into it so deeply that he didn't have time for anything else. And it wasn't like we were making any money from the job. I kept trying to get him to ask for an additional fee but he wouldn't do it. I couldn't understand that. It wasn't like Mrs. Addison didn't have the money. Hell, she could have sold the Eakins and had enough money for two lifetimes."

"What was the painting?"

"Oh, I don't remember."

"William Rush Carving the Allegorical Schuylkill?"

"Yeah, possibly."

"She did sell it," said Ramsgill. "To Harold Farber. For next to nothing."

"She what?" said Farr.

Ramsgill looked up, realizing he was coming up fast on a slow-moving truck. He moved into the passing lane.

"Tell me something," said Ramsgill. "When David was working for the Addisons, did he spend a lot of time out at the house?"

"Of course he did. You know what it takes to do a restoration project. Endless measurements and sketches of existing conditions, probing of the structure, that sort of thing."

"And he was given free reign of the house? Alone sometimes?"

"Well, I assume. The Addisons had their shop in the city. They were there during the day. What are you getting at?"

"I'm not sure. How about David and Harold Farber? Did the two of them see much of each other in those days?"

"I don't know what you mean."

"Would you call them friends?"

"Farber was more of a mentor to David, Jamie. Though I would have to say that Farber did ask for David's advice on matters of taste. David helped him from time to time in furnishing his house and decorating."

"How about in buying art?"

"I don't know about that."

"All right," said Ramsgill. "Look, Tod, this is beginning to make sense and I—"

"Just a minute, Jamie."

There was a moment of silence before Farr came back.

"Another call, Jamie. I've got to take it. Get back to me later on. Do you have my home phone?"

"Yes."

"All right, I'll talk to you soon."

Ramsgill hung up, thinking about what he had learned. He decided to call Anne Holden, Mrs. Addison's niece, at the number Cate had given him. He introduced himself as Cate Chew's brother-in-law, which seemed to give him some credibility. But when he mentioned the Eakins painting it was as though he had just doused her with a bucket of cold water. She withdrew into herself, and it was all he could do to get her to talk to him. She wouldn't agree to meet with him, though she did say that he could call her back in the evening, when she might reconsider. There was nothing he could do, so he hung up.

He phoned the Marilyn Foster Gallery.

"Elena?"

"*Ciao*, love." It was her, but from her muted voice he could tell that Marilyn was within earshot. Marilyn Foster ran her gallery like the

Gestapo, and personal telephone calls generally were not tolerated.

"What's up?"

"Nothing. Marilyn's got Steve Estock in, going over his new show. I'm licking stamps for the invites. An exciting afternoon." She hesitated for a moment before speaking again. "Cate says you didn't have your interview."

"No. David had to . . . well, he's out of the office."

"And you're not coming to dinner?"

"Uh-uh."

"What are you up to, Jamie?"

"I'm doing something for Tod Farr. David's partner."

"What?"

"I can't tell you. But I'll be home later on. Besides, Michael's not coming to dinner anyway."

"Jamie, we have to talk. Cate and I are tired of playing referee between you and Michael. He said he was sorry."

"To Cate, he said he was sorry. To me, he never says anything."

"Jamie, give him the benefit of the doubt, won't you?"

"I've been giving him the benefit of the doubt for—"

"You have not," she cut in. "You've been carrying a chip around on your shoulder ever since he left home. Because he chose to live with your father instead of your mother and you."

Ramsgill's lips squeezed in like a sponge.

"Were you around, Elena? If memory serves me, that was thirty years ago. So how could you know?"

"Don't get mad at me, Jamie. That just proves the point."

"It proves nothing," he snapped. "This is bullshit, Elena."

The line went silent, and Ramsgill's ears fished for sound, knowing now that he had overstepped his bounds.

"Elena?"

She didn't answer, letting the silence draw out like a kite string.

"I have to go," she finally said.

He didn't say anything, and then he realized he had let too much time pass to apologize. It would sound contrived now, like he didn't mean it. He said good-bye and listened for a response, but she hung up without saying a word.

It was nearly five fifteen when David Laycutt pulled into the little clearing in front of his mountain house.

The house was made up of three interconnected pieces, a high central section defined by columns made of lodge pole pines, and two lower sections, like the side aisles of a Gothic church. It was long like a church too, though not nearly so big, situated laterally to a cascading brook and built with wide expanses of glass to take advantage of the views. The exterior was made entirely of cedar shingles and trim, and though angular in conception and bold in design, it looked as though it truly belonged in the clearing. It formed an L with an old shingled barn, which Laycutt used as a studio in the summer.

Laycutt pulled the car around to the side of the house, out of view of the drive. He cut the engine and picked up the briefcase from the seat beside him. As he entered the side door off the kitchen he was met by the stale scent of wet ash, and he realized that he must have left the fireplace damper open the last time he had been here. Inside the house was frigid, and he quickly turned up the thermostat in the hall.

He paused when he reached the long slate counter that separated the kitchen from the living room, setting down the briefcase and the box of cartridges that he carried in his gloved hands. He removed his gloves. He then pulled Ray Paskiewicz's gun from his briefcase, inadvertently tugging at Major Devero's letter which was still in there too. He set down the gun and unfolded the letter. He had already read it a half dozen times, but he began from the beginning, concentrating on Devero's every word.

I'll be brief.

Twenty years is a long time. You have certainly done okay for yourself, and Farber never had to worry about money. I, on the other hand, have hovered just above the plane of obscurity, and frankly I'm weary. I now know what I did for you and Farber was fraudulent, and I don't want to turn you in. But I also know that you profited from my facsimile. I think it only fair that I get some additional compensation. I am requesting a payment of $75,000, in cash, delivered here at 7:30 P.M. on Tuesday, March 26. If you consider this an idle threat, then you have no understanding of my resolve. You have far more to lose than me.

Major

Laycutt stared at the paper, his stomach churning into butter. The letter was composed on a computer, and unsigned. The writing was articulate and to the point, two qualities that Major Devero had always possessed. The tone of the letter was not spiteful, and bitter only in the sense of Devero's admissions of his own failings, with none of that bitterness directed at Laycutt and Farber. Laycutt realized that it was different for Devero, a black man without the social connections necessary to insure success, no matter what kind of talent he possessed. But Laycutt's affection for Devero as a person didn't lessen the blow of Devero's demand. In fact, it almost made it worse, like a parent deceived by a child. Laycutt wadded up the letter and threw it at the fireplace. It caromed off the wall and rolled under a coffee table.

"Fuck you," he blurted.

He opened the box of cartridges and popped out the ammunition clip as Paskiewicz had shown him. He began to slide bullets into the clip. He considered where he and Farber had gone wrong. He never thought that Devero would come forward, at least not with a black-mail threat, and certainly not after all this time. No more than he thought Mrs. Addison would come forward, and there he had been right. Even after she realized that her Eakins was a fake, and that it was probably Laycutt who had arranged the switch of the real painting for Devero's forgery, she never went public with the news. By doing so, she realized, she would be revealing her own secret, one from long ago. And she had had no idea that Harold Farber was Laycutt's accomplice, that much Laycutt was sure of. Otherwise she never would have sold him the forgery.

But Devero was another matter. Laycutt had thought at first that Devero really believed his and Farber's story about why they wanted the facsimile painted. That's what they had called it back then, a facsimile, as if the moniker would give the work some legitimacy. Even if Devero found out about their plot later on, then Laycutt had always assumed that he could threaten him simply by saying that they would tell the authorities that he was an accomplice, dragging him down with them. In hindsight, Laycutt could see that he had been wrong. Devero wouldn't fall for his bluff. And Laycutt did have far more to lose than he did.

Laycutt popped the clip back into the gun and eased off the safety. He looked at the gun as if it were an implement from another place and time, as if it were not in his hand at this confused moment. He wondered what a bullet to the head would feel like, how quickly death would come. He thought of his parents, and, were they still alive, of what they would think of him now when after climbing to the heights of his profession, he had slumped so low. He wondered whether it was all worth it, whether his life could ever be the same.

He raised the gun slowly, and held it out in front of him, his elbows locked, his bloodshot eyes staring down the sights. He made a child-like noise, a soft pow, popping out his cheeks. His heart was pounding now, sluicing blood to every extremity of his being. Suddenly, he flinched, jerking the gun around toward the sliding glass doors at the living room deck. Was that a noise he heard? He held the gun still for a moment, noticing the slight shake of his hand. He then turned the gun so the barrel pointed toward his own head.

"I'll blow you away, bastard," he said, his voice a pale affectation of a film noir gangster.

And then he began to laugh. It was absurd, the whole thing, and he knew it.

In the distance, Jamie Ramsgill could see the first line of mountains, stretching along the gray horizon like a jagged curtain of mauve. The mountains brought back memories of childhood, of day trips for skiing that he, Michael, and his dad had taken, before Michael had left home, before his mother and father had split up. Now it was hard to imagine the four of them as a family, with his father dead and his mother married to a man Ramsgill hardly knew.

At the end of a long downgrade Ramsgill's car approached the Lehigh Tunnel. He was now in a landscape far removed from the city and points further south. Whereas daffodils had been in bloom in Rittenhouse Square, the fields that flanked the highway in this part of the state were still covered with snow. The snow was splotchy on south-facing slopes, like a cake that hasn't quite been iced. But it would be weeks before the snow was fully gone.

Exiting the tunnel north of the mountain, the landscape changed further still. The land rose up in every direction, while beneath the steel span on which he was traveling, the rapid spring waters of the Lehigh River cut deeply into the earth. Lines of still leafless hardwoods ran up steep hillsides like so many matchsticks, interrupted only by bold protrusions of gray rock and more snow. Ramsgill had decided to continue north to Laycutt's mountain house, which was another twenty miles ahead at the edge of the Birch Run State Forest. He would then return to Jim Thorpe, which was just five miles to the west.

By five thirty the sun was dropping behind the mountains, and a cold night was settling in. Cloud cover had moved into the area, and the only decent radio signal Ramsgill could pick up, Country 97 out of Wilkes-Barre, was predicting snow showers in the mountains. He exited the turnpike at White Haven, stopping at a diner for a sandwich and a cup of coffee. The place was almost empty. The few patrons—an old trucker, a father and his teenage daughter, a black state trooper—ate in silence, their vacant stares never meeting one another, almost as if they were inhabitants of a modern-day Edward Hopper painting. Ramsgill ordered and ate his food silently, then remembered he'd not called Cate to cancel dinner for sure. He phoned the house but got no answer. He then tried Michael's law firm, but was told Michael wasn't in. He wondered if Michael really had to work that night, or whether he had made up the story to avoid dinner with him.

By the time Ramsgill was back on the road, it had indeed begun to snow. The road curved like a sidewinder snake, and was narrow, hemmed in by trees. The ground was covered by dense, leafless hardwoods whose feet rested in white. On the forest floor silhouettes of mountain laurel and rhododendron made it impossible to see more than a few feet into the woods. Just south of Tannery a pair of deer leapt in front of the car, jarring him from a momentary lapse of concentration. The blur of white tails disappeared into the brush with an almost surreal suddenness, leaving only an afterburn in the dusk.

At a certain point the road reached its highest elevation and began to descend. It was a constant downgrade as it came into the village of Birch Run, a settlement of no more than three or four houses and a general store. He soon crossed Birch Run itself, a tributary of the Lehigh. At the second road to the right, he turned, and he followed a new road even further downward until it crossed another stream. By now his side window had begun to fog, and he had opened it halfway. As the car's tires lumbered over the wooden trestles of a small bridge, he could hear gurgling water working its way over rocks.

Just past the bridge three mailboxes stood sentry at the entrance to another road. This one was private, and it had not been cleared of ice. He turned the car, spinning past a small pink house on his right and a depressing green trailer next door. Both places were empty, and from the look of it, they had been so for most of the winter. Fifty yards ahead the road ended. An even smaller access way turned off at that point, the driveway, if it could be called that, to Laycutt's house.

Ramsgill parked at the end of the drive, blocking it. If Laycutt were at the house, this would make it impossible for him to leave. On the drive north Ramsgill had been postulating, trying to make some sense of what he knew about Laycutt's disappearance. He was convinced that his friend was being blackmailed by Major Devero, and he thought he knew why. It was the inconsistencies that nagged at him, however, the things he couldn't pigeonhole. Like why the blackmail demand had come in the form of a letter and why Mrs. Addison had never suspected Laycutt or turned him in. And a new one he had just postulated, which had to do with why Devero had chosen to come forward only now.

Ramsgill shut the car door, the sound almost instantly absorbed by the cottony flakes. The scent of evergreen permeated the stillness, and in the near distance the hushed tones of the brook could be heard. Beneath the dusting of new snow and in the shadowless gray of dusk, he could just make out a single set of tire tracks on the drive.

He began walking downhill. He had no idea how he would convince Laycutt not to go through with the payoff, and even less of an idea why he was doing it in the first place. But he kept walking, toward the house, which he could now just barely spot through the trees to the right of the drive. The cold nipped at his fingers and penetrated through his light jacket to his chest. Ahead of him, the drive curved to the right, and it was not so much the dark figure of the house itself that he could see, but rather the light coming from inside. As he turned the corner and the trees opened up, a small flat clearing came into view. Laycutt's house stood at the far end of the clearing, bundled against the edge of the woods, one side facing the stream. The house was rustic yet modern, a painfully thin box dominated by a continuous clearstory, light bounding out of many windows into the surrounding spider web of tree branches.

As he approached he realized that Laycutt's car wasn't in front of the house. Was it on the other side, or perhaps parked in the old barn just beyond? He slowed, the muffled crunch of ice beneath his leatherheeled loafers signaling his pace. He didn't want to scare Laycutt, who was undoubtedly in a fragile state of mind. Ramsgill now wondered whether he should have driven his car up the drive. At least that way Laycutt would have known he was coming. He looked back, back down the drive, then brought his hands to his mouth to warm them. It was too late for that now.

He reached the small wooden front porch and knocked at the door. Getting no answer, he knocked again, suddenly having a premonition. Again no answer, so he used the key Farr had given him. He opened the door and stepped cautiously inside. He flipped a light switch which illuminated the high vaulted clearstory overhead. The hall was demarcated by a line of columns on either side that stretched like telephone poles right up to the roof.

"David?" he called. The question rebounded in silence. He quietly clicked the door behind him, then called again.

"David? It's me. Jamie. Jamie Ramsgill."

No answer, so he moved forward carefully, still cognizant of Laycutt's state of mind. The high narrow hall opened up to the major living spaces, dark beyond the limits of the hall's light. He fumbled for a light switch against a paneled kitchen wall, and when he found it, he turned it on. The kitchen, living, and dining areas were all one space, and they were empty. Ahead of him on a dark stone countertop Ramsgill could see a small box, and he moved toward it with care. When he reached the box he realized that it was a box of ammunition, and again his premonition came to fore.

"David!"

He quickly crossed the living room and swung open a door. The bedroom was empty. Back in the front hall another door, another empty bedroom. He scaled a ladder stair to the sleeping loft, but it too was vacant. He clambered back down, confused. Where the hell was he? He hurried to the sliding glass doors, which opened to the deck. He turned on the deck lights and looked out, but there were no footprints in the snow. A round table and four chairs were blanketed in white. Back in the kitchen, he went through to the small mudroom and to a side door that faced the old barn. He turned on the porch light there, and stared out into the illuminated landscape.

Laycutt's car wasn't there. And it wasn't in the barn either, because Ramsgill could see that it had been parked in the space between the house and the barn, where the single set of tire tracks had ended. Or perhaps started. He now realized that there was but one set of tracks because Laycutt had arrived at the house before it had started snowing, and that he had left within the last half hour.

"Dammit," he whispered.

He returned to the kitchen and spotted the phone and answering machine on the counter. He played a single message.

"Hello. David? This is Harold Farber. I don't know if you're there, but Vibeke told me that a person named Jamie Ramsgill is looking for you. If you get this message, I'll be at the hospital until around three. After that I'll be at the club, that's the Philadelphia Athletic Club, until six. I'm then having dinner with some friends and should be home later. Hope everything is okay. Vibeke said you didn't sound too well. Anyway, give me a call. I suppose we should talk about things."

Ramsgill looked at his watch. It was nearly six fifty-five.

He still wanted to speak to Farber, but there was no time for that now. Laycutt had a gun, and if he wasn't going to kill himself then Ramsgill could guess what he was going to do with it. He took a notepad from next to the phone and started writing. He left Laycutt a note saying that he was driving over to Jim Thorpe. If he didn't find him there, he wrote, then he would return to the cabin, and if Laycutt came back, would he please wait for him. He only wanted to talk, Ramsgill wrote, and he was worried that David might do something he'd regret.

Jamie set the note out at the end of the counter in plain view. He was about to leave when he spotted something on the living room floor, balled up beneath a coffee table.

Up until now Ramsgill had undoubtedly seen David Laycutt as a victim. His well-known friend had always been personable, perhaps even more so as he gained fame—less bitter, more appreciative of everything he had achieved. He had scaled the peak of the ruthlessly competitive world of international architecture, and his work, as well as work ethic, was sincere and inspiring.

But as Ramsgill unrolled the letter and read it, he realized something else. David Laycutt was a desperate man. And his desperation confirmed what Ramsgill supposed he had secretly been denying up to that point.

Laycutt was also a criminal.

The letter stated that Laycutt was to bring the blackmail money to Devero's house at seven thirty on March 26. Ramsgill again looked at his watch. It was exactly seven o'clock. He didn't need to look at a calendar to know that it was March 26.

He smoothed out the letter, folded it twice, and slipped it in the pocket of his jacket. As he rushed for the front door he realized that he had thirty minutes. Thirty minutes to stop David Laycutt from making the mistake of his life.

And thirty minutes to keep Major Devero alive.

Six

*M*ajor Devero stood back from the canvas, the squint in his right eye confirming what his brain was telling him. The painting before him, a small, precise townscape of hard-edged buildings and soft landscape forms, refused to come into harmony. For some reason the Alizarin Crimson he had just applied to the Lehigh Coal and Navigation Building in the foreground of the painting seemed to be orange, even though he had toned the red way down. What was it that made it appear to be that way, he wondered. The Yellow Ochre of the street lamps, perhaps?

Devero had been a painter his entire adult life. Save a two-year stint with the army in the late sixties, he had plied his trade (he liked to think of it as a *trade*—after all, the great artists of the Renaissance had thought of it as such) seven days a week since graduating the Pennsylvania Academy of the Fine Arts in 1967. He painted virtually every day of the year. He thought nothing of rising from bed and walking over to a canvas in progress, before breakfast, before dressing. It wasn't necessarily that he enjoyed it so much, but rather it was a part of life itself. To him it was no different than breathing—rhythmic, regenerative, compulsory.

He had tried not to paint once or twice a long time ago, at moments when his career seemed to be going nowhere. But he inevitably came back, because he found it impossible to sit in his house with paint and canvas that was not being used. It was the difficulty of painting that had always driven him to do it, that, and the beauty of unlocking the simple mysteries of the juxtapositions of form and color. He knew that it had something to do with the boundary between making something appear real (or at least recognizable), while at the same time creating a synthesized view of the world. One had to develop an analog vision, a way of realizing objects not as they ought to appear, but rather as they *have* to appear, given the limitations of the materials. And it was color that still, after all these years, made him lose sleep at night. In his frequent dreams of painting, the colors never remained constant. As soon as a particular pigment would be worked by brush or knife into a canvas, it would begin to metamorphosize, vibrating into a hundred other colors. As he tried to tame it by piling more and more of the original pigment on top of that which had gone before, the vibrations only got worse, until, some nights, he would wake up in a cold sweat, not knowing whether to laugh or to cry, or to simply give up because of the insanity of it all.

"Fine," he said, his mind back in his little studio. He set down a Filbert brush and looked over to a pair of tabby cats named Saguaro and Bull, who were sprawled out on the threadbare hook rug in the middle of the room. He gave them a sardonic grin to let them know that the remark was not directed their way. Major Devero was a slender man with a pleasant face and a smile that his mother had always said could make the devil turn good. His graying hair was cropped short, receding up a shiny brown forehead. He had a thin salt-and-pepper mustache. Hard drinking had etched deep though even lines into his face, accelerating what anyone would guess as his age to be far beyond his fifty-three years.

"Fine," he said again. "Orange? Red? Hell, it could be purple. Doesn't matter."

He picked up a glass of scotch that rested precariously at the edge of his painting materials and threw back his head, tossing the liquid down his throat. Sitting on a paint-splattered wooden stool, he stared at the painting and pretended to smile, as if he were expecting the canvas to apologize. It didn't matter, he told himself again. Quit fretting over a detail that means nothing to the slob who'll buy this thing. You're a hack, Devero, and this painting might as well have been done on black velvet.

It hadn't always been this way. When he first moved to Jim Thorpe in 1973, he had come expecting to do serious painting. He wanted to paint the kind of urban landscapes that had so fascinated the painters he looked to for inspiration, people like John Sloan and Francis Speight. For two years, bolstered by his Farber Fellowship, he was able to do just that. Without the pressure to sell his work, he immersed himself in an investigation of the dialectic between man and nature, with the townscape of Jim Thorpe at its core. His work back then sought to mitigate between the disorder of land forms and the order of the man-made, for which Jim Thorpe was a more than suitable prospect. Somewhat abstract, *The Philadelphia Inquirer* had characterized Devero's early paintings as being as interesting as anything Wayne Thibaud was doing in San Francisco, and Thibaud, after all, was represented by a major New York gallery and had put on several one-man shows. In a 1974 "People to Watch in the Arts" article, the *Inquirer* suggested that soon Devero would be a major star.

Devero believed it, but like much of what he aspired to in his career, it never happened. He found that the art world, like so many others, revolved around who one knew and one's gender and ethnicity. It was an exclusionary club, and, at least in those days, almost completely dominated by white males. Whenever he told someone that he was a painter, he found that he had to add parenthetically *a painter of pictures and not houses.*

Not only did Devero not become a star, but he never even got a New York show. When the fellowship money dried up, he found it difficult to make a living from painting. Destined not to give in, however, he gradually drifted toward realism. As Jim Thorpe started to transform itself from coal to tourism, he began to sell scenes of the town to tourists. He soon found himself composing pictures not by any interest suggested by the forms of his subject matter, but rather by which landmarks he had to include in order for the paintings to sell, or how large a painting had to be to look comfortable over a sofa.

In 1976, an old acquaintance, David Laycutt, came to him with an intriguing proposition. Harold Farber, their former patron, was interested in buying a facsimile of a painting, and not just any painting, but a version of Thomas Eakins' *William Rush Carving His Allegorical Figure of the Schuylkill River.* Farber would pay Devero $20,000 to make the copy, but it had to be an exact replica, and it would have to be completed in ten days. Laycutt appealed to Devero's ego, telling him that Farber would entrust the assignment to no one else, because he felt that no other painter was up to the task. He also appealed to Devero's financial situation, which he knew was not good.

Laycutt brought along $5,000 in cash as a down payment for the work. If Devero were interested, Laycutt told him, then he could keep the down payment. Upon completion, and Farber's approval, Devero would get the additional $15,000. But he must swear to never tell anyone what he had done.

At that request, Devero looked at Laycutt with suspicion.

"Why?" he asked.

"Harold's playing a joke on someone," said Laycutt. "An expensive joke, but he still has to have your promise that you won't say anything."

Laycutt's hand rested on an envelope, within which was the down payment. It was a thick envelope that looked not unlike a miniature pillow. Devero thought about his mortgage payment, and about his sister in Philadelphia. Bernice wanted to go to the cosmetology institute, but she didn't have the money. Five thousand dollars, with promise of another fifteen, would go a long way.

"What are you really going to do with it?" Devero asked.

"For God's sake, we're talking twenty thousand dollars, Major."

Devero hesitated, then gave in.

"All right," he said. "But ten days is not enough time. I haven't copied a painting since I was at the academy. It's not easy, and we used to have the actual paintings to work from. It'll be difficult working from photographs."

"You won't have to use photographs," said Laycutt. "I'll be back next Monday. With the real thing."

For a moment Devero thought that he hadn't heard Laycutt correctly. Where the hell was he going to get the real thing? Steal it from a museum?

He found out a week later. Laycutt and the painting arrived as promised. When the canvas was unveiled, Devero could see immediately that *this* version was not one of the ones from a museum. It was one he had never seen. If he hadn't known better, and if he weren't being paid $20,000 to copy it, then he would have thought it was a fake.

Laycutt also brought along photographs of the painting, "just in case" Devero needed them. He told Devero that he could work on the painting for more than ten days if necessary, but that he would have to work from photographs after Laycutt retrieved the real painting by the following Thursday. As it turned out, Devero never needed the photographs, nor the full ten days. He finished his copy by Thursday morning, having worked on it for nearly three days without sleep. In the process he realized that he had an aptitude for this kind of work, and he took extreme care to produce verisimilitude. He envisioned himself and Eakins tied together as soulmates, as neither of them had ever had a New York dealer or a one-man show.

He worked on old canvas, taken from a roll he had once found in the basement of the academy. He made stretchers from aged boards pulled from the shed in his backyard, nailed together by rusting wire brads. He studied every brush stroke on the original, figuring out just what layers of which colors had gone on first, and how certain areas had been reworked. Like Eakins, he laid down the color broadly in thin layers, then built it up in successive overpainting and glazes. He blended in Oil of Spike Lavender in heavy amounts, and used a hair dryer to dry the paint, accelerating the process of crackleature, the creation of tiny fissures on the surface, to make it appear older. He used a spray bottle filled with dirty water to antique the facsimile, and cold-pressed linseed oil to produce a yellow overtone. He even made a coal fire in the backyard and suspended the painting above it, to give it a patina of soot, and to dry out the paint, eliminating the odor of newness.

When Laycutt returned, Devero stood the two paintings on adjacent easels, and he watched silently, as for a full two minutes Laycutt moved from one painting to the other, comparing details but never saying a word.

"Jesus," he said, as he finished. He turned to Devero and smiled, the ends of his mouth almost coming into contact with his ears.

"Like it?" said Devero.

"Like it? It's uncanny. I'll have to admit, Major, even though Farber was sold on the idea of having you do this, I wasn't so sure. I think our only problem now is that it might be a bit *too* perfect."

Devero grinned, his broad mouth letting out bursts of deep laughter.

"Too perfect?" he said.

Even though Devero was a tall man, he still found himself looking up to the artist. Laycutt cleared his throat.

"Yes. For Farber's joke to work, we need some detail that's a little off. Something that, however subtle, might allow it to be construed as a fake."

"No need to worry," Devero said. "I've taken care of that. I still have enough of an ego to keep one clue as to the fact that I painted it. I couldn't give that up."

Laycutt again stared at the two paintings.

"I don't see it," he said. "What's different?"

"After you came here last week, I did some reading on Eakins. He once wrote that his aim in art was to recreate a moment in time with as much realism as is humanly possible. You can see in the painting how far he goes. The clothes of the lady, for instance, are perfect for the early nineteenth century, as are Rush's. And look at the chair the clothes are draped on. No, not on my copy. On the original."

"It's a Chippendale chair," said Laycutt.

"Now look at mine," said Devero.

"It's also a Chippendale."

"But they're not the same. Mine is more characteristic of New England Chippendale. Like I said, Eakins was a stickler for detail. His has rounded rear legs and exposed mortises in the back. If there's one thing I remember from art history classes about early American furniture, it was that each city had its own slight variation from Chippendale's original chairs, the ones in Thomas Chippendale's book. Eakins put a genuine Philadelphia chair in his picture. Mine has square rear legs, and a different back splat. And my side rails are straight. I copied it from a book on works at the Museum of Fine Arts, Boston."

"Clever," said Laycutt. "And I suppose an art historian would know the difference?"

"Any historian that knew Eakins' work would. Though you've got to look extremely carefully to see the difference. It's like one of those exercises kids do, you know, *What's different in these two pictures?*"

Laycutt nodded, and Devero could tell he was pleased. He took the painting and a week later Devero received the balance of his payment. The twenty thousand was more money than Devero normally made in a year, and it had taken him but two weeks to get it. He gave five thousand to his sister Bernice, and a bit more to his mother, who by then, was living in a home. The rest he kept in savings. It was his rainy day money, but eventually he went through it all. Which is why he was excited now, and why he rose from the stool.

"Daddy needs another drink," he said to the cats. He loped across the carpet and the two felines sprang out of his way. He made his way to the kitchen and fixed himself another drink, mostly scotch this time, with just a shot of soda.

Back in the studio, an octagonal-shaped room off the front parlor of his Victorian house, he dropped his brushes into a can of turpentine. All he had to do now was to wait for his appointment. It was snowing lightly outside; it had been so for about an hour. He hoped the roads were clear. He was nervous, but he really didn't think anything would go wrong. Things had gone so smoothly twenty years ago. Why would they be different now?

Suddenly out the front window he saw a car slow in front of the house, its red taillights pulsing momentarily before pulling further up the hill. Devero had made sure to park his truck far enough up his driveway so there would be room for two cars, as there was no parking on the street anywhere near his house. He thought he had mentioned that, but perhaps he was wrong. He looked down at his watch, which was an old Seiko that kept perfect time, but which, like most of his personal effects, had not been left unscathed by paint. Beneath the splattered crystal he could see that it was seven twenty. He took another belt of scotch before turning off the lights in the studio. He went into the front parlor, straightening a pile of newspapers on the sofa and putting the throw pillows back in their place. A few moments later, he heard hard-soled shoes on the wooden floorboards of the front porch. Not only had the roads been clear, but his appointment was ten minutes early.

The doorbell rang and Devero set his drink down on an end table next to the sofa. When he reached the front door Saguano already had pushed her body against it, an old trick of hers to get herself picked up. She knew Devero couldn't answer the door without moving her first, and as he loved his cats, it meant that he usually lifted and stroked her, while welcoming visitors.

He did exactly that. He cradled her under his arm while shifting the lace curtains of the glass viewing panel to one side. Looking out, he nodded as he combed her back with his finger, and she looked up at him and winked. He turned the door's glass knob and pulled it towards him, stepping out of the way.

Seven

*R*amsgill exited the turnpike and took 209 south, a winding two-lane perched well above the waters of the Lehigh. As he headed west it was as though he were driving into a romantic landscape painting from the nineteenth century, something from the Hudson River School. Even in near darkness he could see the succession of mountains folding down into the valley like so many ocean waves, disappearing against the black slab of the river.

The snow was falling lightly now. Shortly the road curved north and at a broad bend in the river, he could see the old coal town of Jim Thorpe, formerly known as Mauch Chunk, its small business district nestled into the flats. It looked like a toy village of a model railway set, dominated by three towers and a grand house. The cylindrical turret and broad shed roof of the old Lehigh Valley railroad station stood closest to the river, backed up by the dark, Gothic steeple of St. Mary's Church and the square Romanesque clock tower of the County Courthouse. The illuminated courthouse clock glowed like a fall moon. Each of the three buildings stood at a different elevation, knitted together by a myriad of Victorian facades. Hovering over the entire scene was the Italianate mansion of Asa Packer, former railroad magnate. The house was lit up like a birthday cake, its ornate cupola, porches, and brackets like bits of fancy white icing, shocked by floodlighting that could be seen all the way from the other side of the valley.

Ramsgill drove through town, never losing sight of the brightly lit mansion. Just past the railroad station and the courthouse, he turned left, and began his ascent up a hill.

To call Packer Avenue an avenue was a misnomer, as it was more like a funicular railway without the rails. It climbed straight up the side of a hill that belonged in San Francisco, in fact steeper than anything Ramsgill had ever seen in San Francisco, and out there they rarely had to contend with snow. There were only four houses on the road, all of them on the left, built into the land. To the right a guardrail separated the avenue from the disappearing highway and river below. The last of winter's ice clung to the road shoulder. He climbed past the Packer Mansion itself, with its sign out front offering tours of "Victorian splendor." Next door was the Harry Packer mansion, a mansarded High-Victorian, as eccentric as it was large. Beyond this was a shadowy bungalow that looked to be abandoned. And finally, above them all, situated on a wooded lot, was a two-story red clapboard house, outlined in white trim. It had a porch that wrapped the front and right sides, and an octagonal turret that anchored the corner where the two porches came together. There was no mailbox, but a street number had been painted on a stone in the front yard. It was 41 Packer.

Ramsgill drove slowly past the house, then past an empty wooded lot above it, next door. There the road bore to the left, and as it straightened out again, he crested the steepest portion of the hill. Ahead of him was a plateau of sorts, sloped more moderately, with single rowhouses and Victorian twins on either side of the road. Halfway up the block Ramsgill found a parking spot on his right, between a driveway and a whale-like mound of dirty snow. He stepped silently from the car, conscious of being a stranger in what looked to be a tight-knit neighborhood. He walked slowly downhill past the wooded parcel. When he reached Devero's driveway, he paused to catch his breath.

He could now see that the house stood on a solid stone base and that the unlit porch fronted generous windows that looked in on high-ceilinged rooms. Most of the downstairs rooms were illuminated, with the exception of a room at the base of the octagon, just off the porch. A white Ford pickup was pulled to the end of the driveway, and beyond it several outbuildings stood about a small floodlit backyard.

He was about to climb the driveway when a chilling sensation enveloped him. Feeling something brush across his leg, he looked down and was relieved to see that it was only a cat, a plump creature with orange and white fur, its head nudging his calf.

"Hello," Ramsgill said. "Anybody home?"

He gave the cat a quick rub, then climbed the drive. The cat followed him without hesitation, which made Ramsgill think he belonged to the owner of the house. The drive was packed with ice, a glossy undulating surface that had obviously frozen and thawed a number of times during winter. He crossed over to the front steps, stepping into crunchy snow already criss-crossed with footprints.

On the porch, Ramsgill became aware of the constant whispering *rurr* of the river far below him. He rang the bell, which was next to a glass paneled door, at first tentatively, then again in quick pulses. Through the glass behind a drooping lace curtain, he could see a parlor inhabited only by furniture. He waited for a full minute, but didn't get an answer. He then looked down to the glowing dial of his Swatch. He had made the trip down from Birch Run in just twenty-five minutes, and he now realized he was early. It was seven twenty-five, five minutes before Laycutt's scheduled appointment.

He then left the porch and hurried around the corner of the house. He checked the pickup, which was empty, and walked on to the backyard, at the rear of which was an old garage. It was a board and batten affair, with walls that were cupped and tilting and a roof that looked as though it might cave in any day. But as he pressed his nose and hands against a window situated in an inoperable garage door, he could see that the inside of the garage had been renovated. Its walls had been wainscoted in warm tongue and groove boards, and the floor had been covered in linoleum tile. Several easels stood in different positions about the room, along with a work table covered by sketch pads, books, and painting supplies.

There was no one inside, but something about the work captured his attention. He walked around the side door and entered the garage. He was met squarely by the strong odor of paint and turpentine, effused with the smell of raw wood. He worked his way around two of three easels, finally coming to one that contained something of interest. Two small oil sketches rested in the easel's frame, one a study of the sculptor Benjamin Rush's massive hands from the painting of *Rush Carving*, and the second, a study of the female model's clothes. On a table near the sketches were several books on Eakins, and beneath the pile was a series of color 8 x 10 photos of what Ramsgill assumed was the original painting. A roll of old canvas lay nearby, and a small cardboard box held a hair dryer, some old wire brads, a hammer, a spray bottle full of brown liquid, and a bottle of something called Oil of Spike Lavender. It was obvious what Devero was doing here.

He left the garage and returned to the house's front porch, again looking at his watch, which now read seven thirty. A train whistle broke the silence, slicing through the river valley like a meat cleaver. By now the cat had curled up within the jamb of the doorway, perhaps waiting for her master to open the door and let her in. Ramsgill glanced through the lace curtain again, but this time something was different. He could hardly make out the furniture in the front parlor.

"What the . . . ?" he whispered.

He pressed his nose up to the glass and stared into the room. The only light he could make out now was from a back room, perhaps a kitchen, down a narrow hallway to the right of a stair. Ramsgill remembered seeing the stair before. He also remembered an upholstered sofa covered with newspapers in front of it, and, next to the sofa, a floor lamp. He was sure that, before he had gone to the garage, the floor lamp had been on.

He knocked on the door again, this time loudly and rapidly. When he didn't get an answer, he tried the glass knob.

"Hello?" The echo of his voice resounded through the stillness, getting lost somewhere in the darkness of the high ceiling above him, or perhaps traveling up the open stairway to the second floor.

"Hello? Mr. Devero?"

He stepped forward and the cat ran up between his legs, poking its head tentatively into the space. He shut the door behind him and the glass rattled in its frame.

Ramsgill tried to get his bearings. Ahead of him was the dark hall leading to the back of the house. The kitchen was definitely at the end of the hall, as he could now hear the hum of the refrigerator. Two doors opened off the hall, both dark, and it was hard to tell whether they were open or closed. In the parlor itself he could just make out the stair on the opposite wall. On the left wall, a pair of windows overlooked a side yard. To the right, a wide opening led into another room, the one within the octagonal tower.

Suddenly the cat sprang forward in perfect silence. It tiptoed two or three steps then slowed to a stop, arching its long body to the right, such that its head peered through the opening into the octagonal room. Ramsgill started forward too, not as quietly as the cat, in the direction of the floor lamp that he knew was on the other side of the parlor. As he passed the cat, the cat leapt again, this time going through the opening into the octagon. Just as it came to a second stop, Ramsgill saw something on the floor of the octagonal room, beyond the feline. But before he could tell what it was, his head was rocked by something hard, sending him halfway across the room. Stunned, he tried to pick himself up off the floor. But he was slammed down again, this time ending up in the left corner of the room, back by the stair. With no idea what was before him, he groped to his unsteady feet, turned, and charged to his right. His shoulder met the midsection of a body. A grunt came from the body as he drove it backwards, and then another, as the body smashed into a hard plaster wall. But the body had the object that had hit Ramsgill, whatever it was, and again it was swung down hard against the side of Ramsgill's face. For a split second before impact Ramsgill managed to get a hand on the object, grabbing at what felt like a handle, which slowed it down. The collision still knocked him backwards though, back toward the hall. This time he didn't want to get up. He heaved for breath, wondering whether he should run. But just as he lifted his head he saw the front door fly open and his attacker scramble off the dark porch, away into the night.

He sat motionless while his heart accelerated to catch up with the rapidity of his breathing, his eyes fanning the darkness in belated fear. As his breathing slowed to a more normal rate, he instinctively brought his hand up to his cheek, which felt three times its normal size. He shook his head—the wrong thing to do, as the pain inside screamed out for relief.

He rose and fumbled in the darkness until he found the floor lamp. He turned it on, and the light hit him as if he had been asleep. He squinted through the brightness at the parlor. There was a hole in the wall next to the octagonal room doorway, and bits of plaster on the floor.

Just then he noticed something next to him. He looked down to see the object that had hit him, which he had somehow managed to wrangle free during the melee. It was a black leather briefcase with brass locks. He knelt down and opened it, and inside he found scores of hundred-dollar bills, banded into packets of $5,000 each.

The cat purred in the other room. Ramsgill shut the briefcase and stood, then walked toward the open doorway. His head felt like a sponge full of water, and he could feel warm blood coming from above his right eye. As he stepped into the room his path was barred by an object on the floor. He flipped on the light switch to the right of the door, and there before him was a man. He was lying on his stomach with his head turned to one side. He wore a baggy gray sweatshirt and old jeans, topsiders and white socks. Ramsgill noticed that the socks were the only part of the man unscathed by paint. The jeans, the sweatshirt, and the shoes were splotched in blue and green, yellow and orange, red and purple. Ramsgill even thought for a second that the back of the man's head had been splattered, until he realized that the bright red mark there was blood, a pool of which had soaked into an old rug beneath him.

The orange and white cat was perched before the figure, its front legs at attention, its buttocks glued to the floor. Another cat, this one mostly black, lay on the rug behind the first one. Ramsgill walked around to the side of the body and the cats scampered off, settling into shadowed corners of the studio. He peered down at the man. The moment he saw the face he recognized it. It was the man from the photograph he had seen at Laycutt's apartment, the man on the right in the picture, who like Laycutt had received a fellowship from Harold Farber. A lack of pulse confirmed that he was dead.

So this was Major Devero, he thought.

He knelt down, blind-sided again, this time by guilt.

He had done nothing to stop this from happening, and he now realized that Tod Farr notwithstanding, they should have called in the police from the beginning. Major Devero would still be alive, and David Laycutt wouldn't be a murderer.

Ramsgill looked to his side, realizing his fingers still gripped the briefcase. He popped it open again and quickly counted the packets of money. There were ten of them in all, making a total of $50,000. He had to stop and think for a moment, wondering if the blows to his head had affected his memory. He was sure that Devero's letter had demanded $75,000. He was also sure that Tod Farr had told him Laycutt withdrew $75,000 from the firm's bank account. What had happened to the other $25,000? Had Laycutt tried to short Devero? And then he remembered something else. For the brief second he had gotten a glimpse of his attacker as he ran out Devero's front door, he thought he saw something under his arm. It wasn't the briefcase though, at least not this one. It was a bigger object. Had there been two briefcases, the second one larger, containing the other $25,000?

Ramsgill stood and turned to a painting on an easel in the middle of the room. It was a scene of Jim Thorpe, skillfully painted but sentimental in tone. He walked around the easel to the far corner of the room where several more canvases leaned against a wall. They were all scenes of the town, architectural in nature. Some of them had stickers on the back, with seven hundred and fifty dollars being about the average price. Each of the pictures was highly detailed, and Ramsgill figured each must have taken a considerable effort to produce. Not an easy way to make a living, he thought.

Ramsgill pulled the letter from the pocket of his jacket and looked at it again. It clearly implicated not only Laycutt, but also Farber, in a plot to defraud someone. In Ramsgill's mind that someone was Mrs. Addison. He figured that it probably started innocently enough, Laycutt working on his very first commission, young and idealistic, right after starting his firm. Farr had told Ramsgill that he personally never had to worry about money, but that in the early days of the firm Laycutt had. So Laycutt begins working for the Addisons and Mr. Addison dies. Mrs. Addison turns out to be rather loopy. She drinks, she makes inconsistent decisions, she changes her mind, she requires more of Laycutt's time on the job than he had anticipated. The longer he's into it the less he can extricate himself, and the more the job drains on the firm. He didn't ask for an additional fee, Farr had told Ramsgill, which meant that in effect he was working on the job gratis. Since he was spending so much time on Mrs. Addison's job, that was time he presumably couldn't spend on profitable work.

But how did the painting come into it all? Mrs. Addison must have acquired the painting during the time that Laycutt was working for her. And as Laycutt would have spent a great deal of time at the house, he undoubtedly came to know what the painting was, and its value. Something, financial problems or whatever, caused him to concoct the plan to take the painting. He had a contact in Major Devero to paint a facsimile, who perhaps by that time was already struggling himself. But he would have had to have paid Devero: enter Harold Farber. He then only needed Mrs. Addison out of the house long enough to make the switch. He would replace the original with Devero's facsimile, and Farber would get the original. What does Laycutt get? A finder's fee from Farber to help pay off his debts? The promise to split the profits if Farber was to sell the painting after Mrs. Addison died?

Ramsgill turned back to Devero's body, now feeling nervous to be in the house.

But there were still gaps, he thought. First of all, how could Devero have painted a facsimile with such accuracy that Mrs. Addison did not recognize the forgery immediately? Cate had said that Mrs. Addison had a consummate eye. Devero could have worked from photographs like the ones he had seen in the garage, but photographs never communicate the right balance of color in a work of art. And even more perplexing, why didn't Mrs. Addison suspect Laycutt of having made the switch, once it was determined that Devero's forgery had taken the place of her real painting? And why would Farber buy the forgery from her a few years later, when he knew full well that it wasn't real?

Ramsgill's heart was beginning to beat a little faster now. He realized that he should either call the police or get out of there, or both. He walked back to the parlor, his eyes and ears now wary of the world outside Devero's house.

Then, quite simply, one of the questions answered itself. The plan had perfect symmetry. Farber obviously had bought the fake from Mrs. Addison so he could destroy it, thus destroying any evidence of the plot against her. He already had possession of the real painting, which Laycutt had gotten for him, and which he could hold onto until she died. Then it's reappraised post-mortem, and voilá, suddenly it's an original. An original worth several million dollars, obtained for whatever he paid Devero and Laycutt in the first place, and the few hundred dollars he paid Mrs. Addison later to take the forgery off her hands. But why would she sell it to him? Did she have no idea he was involved?

Ramsgill walked back into the studio. He looked around him, trying to find an answer, as if it might be waiting for him there, sitting on the shelf.

He picked up the briefcase, wondering what he should do with the money. If he let the police have it then it would become state's evidence at trial against Laycutt. And half of it was legally Tod Farr's. Actually three-quarters of it, as Laycutt had already done something with the other twenty-five thousand. Ramsgill wondered if Farr would ever get back his share after a trial. It might be used as remuneration for the victim's family, after all, Devero had a sister.

Just then Ramsgill's ears pricked to the sound of something in the distance. Another train whistle? No. This was different, a siren, intermittent with a squawk. It was growing louder, and then more squawking, coming from a different direction—two police cars were headed for Devero's house.

Ramsgill left the room and in the parlor turned right, then clambered for the kitchen. He stopped suddenly, remembering the briefcase. He hurried back to the studio and grabbed it. His eyes shot laserlike around the room, then without hesitating he left again. He was back in the kitchen and almost out the rear door when he stopped a second time. It was crazy, he knew it, but a voice inside him kept telling him to get rid of the money. In a small closeted area off the back stoop he found a washer and dryer. He dropped the briefcase behind the dryer. He then leapt for the door. Once outside, he winced at the loudness of the sirens. He knew he should stop, just walk down the driveway and give himself up, but it was like someone else was controlling him, a stronger voice, saying *run*. He jumped a low fence that separated Devero's yard from the wooded property next door, oblivious to his footprints in the snow. He ran up through the woods in the direction of the street where his car was parked, soon coming out to the street itself. He cursed himself for having parked in such a dense neighborhood, whose residents would spill out of their houses at any second to see what all the commotion was about. He also cursed David Laycutt, who undoubtedly had phoned in the report of a murder.

By the time he reached the car his breathing was near to hyperventilation. What seemed like hours in reality must have been just seconds, though, because he peeled out of the parking space at the exact point that he saw lights flashing through the trees in the rearview mirror, back downhill near Devero's house. He was almost at the intersection of a cross street by the time the first neighbors came out onto the sidewalk, or at least so he thought. As he approached the stop sign at the corner, a large man stepped out into the street. He was looking downhill towards Devero's house when suddenly he saw Ramsgill barreling for him. He jumped back to the curb, giving Ramsgill the eye. As Ramsgill turned through the intersection without stopping, he again caught sight of the man in his rearview mirror. He was still eyeing Ramsgill's car.

Ramsgill's brakes squealed like a pig being slaughtered as the car completed its descent of the steep hill and came to the highway. A police car cut him off as he started out into traffic, but it didn't stop, instead climbing the hill that Ramsgill had just come down. Ramsgill's fingers gripped the steering wheel like a vise, then he shot out into traffic, turning left. His heart was a raging comet. He was moving too fast to make the quick right turn onto the bridge that crossed the river. Instead he floored it, his foot holding the accelerator down for a full minute, until finally, a mile out of town, he slowed. He eased up on his grip of the steering wheel, his hands trembling, while his mind raced with thoughts of what to do next.

And then he saw them. Red and blue strobes flashing behind him, a half mile back. He was on a road paralleling the river, wedged between steep woods to his left and the water below him on the right. No way to turn, nowhere to go but straight. He thrust down the accelerator again, thinking that he must have lost his mind. He had nothing to hide, and yet here he was running from the law.

What the hell had Laycutt done? He had obviously phoned the police and, from the size of the force that had been dispatched, told them about Devero's murder. He must have also told them that the murderer was still at the house, to try to pin the murder on the person with whom he had struggled. Ramsgill knew that if he gave up he would become a suspect in Devero's killing. He imagined that his face was not very pretty, given that his eye now throbbed. There would be no way of disguising the fact that he had been in a fight, and since Devero was dead, the police would assume the fight had been between the two of them. There was also the briefcase with the money in it, if they found it. His fingerprints were all over it. And maybe elsewhere in the house. And the blackmail letter which he had in his pocket. The letter did not begin with "Dear David," and it never mentioned his name. For all the police knew, it had been written to Ramsgill.

The lights behind him seemed to be gaining. The road was dark and dangerous, and Farr's car bounced up and down wildly. A Jim Thorpe policeman would have been on this road a hundred times, while to Ramsgill it was completely unfamiliar. Ramsgill again shoved the pedal downward, until he thought he would push it through the floorboard.

Up ahead he suddenly saw a reflective yellow sign in the form of a diamond coming for him like a raging buffalo. It was a sign for a T-intersection, a ninety-degree left-hand turn while the main road went straight on. Behind him Ramsgill could still see the flashing strobes, at about the same distance. He decided to make one bold move.

He started braking well before the turn. Despite that, the car still took the turn far too fast and Ramsgill thought he was going to flip. The new road was narrow, shooting up through a gap in the mountains. Once he was out of sight of the police car he turned out his lights. He braked and turned again, backing up once to reverse the car around to face the intersection. He then shot blindly out onto the highway. He floored the car back in the direction of Jim Thorpe, heading straight toward the cop, driving without lights.

It took only a few seconds for the police cruiser's headlights to hit him. Ramsgill flipped on his high beams, heading straight on. The game of chicken ended quickly though, not because Ramsgill outlasted the cop, but because the cruiser tried to brake, to perhaps turn and cut Ramsgill off. But it fishtailed wildly, then jerked back across the road like it had been shot out of a slingshot. It slammed into the guardrail separating the road from an embankment high above the river, and by the time Ramsgill was by it, it had thudded to a stop. Smoke or steam or something blew up from the hood, and the brake lights dimmed to dark. Ramsgill stopped, perhaps a hundred yards beyond where the cop had hit the guardrail. Was he crazy, he wondered? Running from the police was one thing, but killing a cop was another. He was about to put the car into reverse when he saw the cruiser door open and an officer stumble out. He was okay. The cop then reached into the car and pulled out a radio transmitter. Ramsgill again floored his car, spinning off in a tornado of smoke and burnt rubber, realizing that he had to make it to the bridge before the cop dispatched another patrol car. In less than two minutes he had made it to the bridge. In another fifteen minutes he had arrived at the turnpike, but this time, with the police now looking for a red Audi, he didn't get on.

Eight

*I*t was raining by the time Ramsgill got back to the city, the kind of cold insistent drizzle that makes one forget about spring. Traffic on the parkways was moving slowly, each vehicle a multiplicity of light, real and reflected, a kaleidoscopic weave against the misty grid of the Center City skyline. The museum stood atop Fair Mount, glowing a soft pinkish-beige, the color muted by the rain. The boathouses on the river were stitched together with tiny Tivoli lights, twinkling like fireflies in front of a broad horizontal mirror.

Ramsgill had taken the long way home. He had drifted over to Easton at the New Jersey state line, then come down through Bucks County to avoid the turnpike. As far as he was concerned, Tod Farr's bright red Audi might as well have had the sign *murderer* emblazoned across the windshield. He was glad to be back in the city where even if the car was spotted, no one would care enough to do anything about it.

He had tried to telephone Farr on the way. At the home number Farr had given him he got a recording. At the office he spoke to a woman named Margo Baines, Laycutt/Farr's bookkeeper, who was working late. She told him that Farr wasn't in.

"By the way," Ramsgill had said to her, after explaining that Farr had him looking for David Laycutt, "was I right in understanding that David withdrew seventy-five thousand dollars from the bank this morning?"

"Why do you want to know?"

74

"Because that's what Tod told me. I just wanted to make sure that I had my facts right. And that it wasn't fifty thousand."

"It was seventy-five, all right, Mr. Ramsgill. Which is why my sorry behind is here at nine fifteen at night—trying to pull a rabbit out of a hat to keep this firm afloat."

"Okay," said Ramsgill. "If you hear from Tod tonight, would you have him call me? He has my number."

She said that she would and they hung up.

Ramsgill had then tried the number in Bryn Mawr that Anne Holden had given him earlier in the afternoon. This time she was seemingly interested in speaking to someone about her aunt's Eakins painting. She told Ramsgill to come by her shop on Pine Street the next day at nine, when they could discuss it further.

For the rest of the drive he had tried to piece together what he knew. Part of it was cut and dried, like the fact of Devero's blackmailing Laycutt, and of Laycutt's coming after him. Like the motives behind taking the painting in the first place, and how it had probably gone down.

But there was more to it, Ramsgill realized, and that was what gnawed at him. Not to mention that he still had no proof of their plot, save a letter which could have been written to anybody, and a forgery that had probably long since been destroyed.

He exited the Vine Street Expressway at Sixth Street, and headed south past Independence National Historical Park. A few of the carriages that offer tourist rides were parked in front of the Liberty Bell Pavilion, waiting for passengers that on this gloomy night would never come. Beyond the Liberty Bell, Independence Hall stood as an embalmed piece of Colonial America, isolated in a green park. It had always struck Ramsgill as odd that the park's urban planners had razed the older structures surrounding the building, so that it now stood out as a museum piece and not the living building that it had once been.

He found a place to park on Delancy Street, a block away from his brother's house. He had thought about first going to see Harold Farber, but the day had already stretched to twelve hours, and he was tired. He wanted a half dozen ibuprofen, which he planned on washing down with bourbon.

He let himself in and disarmed the security system. He was careful to be quiet, thinking that if the system was on, then everyone must be asleep. He headed straight to the kitchen, "fixed himself a drink," and popped a Chopin CD into the portable disc player on the granite counter. He sat on a stool at the peninsula between the kitchen and family room beyond. His head was pounding and his shoulder hurt now. He sipped his drink quietly, trying to let the soft music seep into his brain. There were some papers on the counter, which he fingered. Mostly legal papers from Michael's office. But even in near darkness he could see that one document was a Complaint that had been served against Michael, prepared by another lawyer. Perhaps it was this Complaint, Ramsgill thought, that had Michael acting like a jerk. Just then Ramsgill thought he heard the creak of footsteps on the stair. He hastily shoved the Complaint back into the pile of papers.

Elena Piruzzi came into the kitchen, wearing nothing but a satin dressing gown. Her hair was loose and her makeup removed, but he could still make out her features. Her eyes lit up the darkness, and her smile almost made him forget what had happened that night. She walked over and wrapped her arms around him, the faint scent of her body odor filling his aural senses.

They held each other in silence, until finally Ramsgill spoke.

"I'm sorry I snapped at you," he said.

"Where have you been?" she said.

He looked up, and his hands moved toward her hair, combing through its silkiness. He then brought the tip of a single finger down the bridge of her nose, ending at her mouth. She pressed her lips to the finger.

"Remember the first time you kissed me?" he said.

"Of course. I did it to make you search Franco Cavalliere's room. At Father's villa."

"That was the only reason you did it?"

"Oh, I liked you. But at the time it was the most expedient thing to do."

He laughed softly, and he realized that they were into their game. Gentle ribbing, all the while feeling the feel of each other's body.

"I thought you liked Franco," he said. "You know, the strong and silent type."

She took his finger between her teeth and pretended to bite down.

"No," she said. "I liked you. The weak and talkative type."

He pulled the finger from her mouth and jabbed it at her ribcage. She squiggled until he pulled her waist back toward him.

"How are you feeling?" he said.

"Tired," she said.

"Too tired to make love?"

"It's one day on, Jamie, and then one day off. Remember?"

Ramsgill smiled to himself. He was lucky to have Elena. When they had first talked about it, he had been reluctant to try to have a child. He now relished the thought, more than anything else in his life.

The lights in the kitchen flicked on, and the two of them looked up startled.

"I'm sorry."

Michael Ramsgill stood on the other side of the room, embarrassed. He was wearing a burgundy jacquard robe with matching slippers.

"It's okay, Michael," said Elena. She smiled at him but he was looking past her with concerned eyes.

"What the hell happened to you?"

Elena looked down to Jamie. In the new light she could see a purple bruise implanted on his swollen left cheek, starting at the protrusion of bone just below the eye socket and running halfway down his jaw. He also had a small cut above his right eyebrow.

"I was attacked."

"Attacked? Where?"

Just then Cate entered the kitchen. She too was dressed for bed. She took one look at Jamie and brought her hand up to her face.

"Upstate," said Jamie. "In Jim Thorpe."

"What were you doing in Jim Thorpe?"

"I went to call on a man named Major Devero. Remember, Cate? I asked you about him this afternoon."

Cate nodded, trying to hold back a yawn.

"Who is he?" she said. Jamie drained the last of his drink. Cate walked out from behind Michael and poured him another bourbon.

"You look like you need this," she said.

"Thanks," he said. "Devero's an artist. And from the looks of things, not a very successful one. He did have one significant commission twenty years ago, though."

"What was that?"

"He painted a facsimile of Eakins' *Rush Carving*."

The look of surprise on Cate's face lasted only a second before it was replaced by consternation.

Jamie continued. "Your Dr. Farber paid him to produce a copy of it. And David Laycutt, my architect friend, probably arranged the whole deal."

"For what purpose?" said Cate.

"Remember how you told me that Mrs. Addison kept the painting for several years, prior to having it appraised?"

Cate nodded.

"Well, that was the same time period that David was working on Mrs. Addison's house. My guess is he switched the forgery for the real painting, before she ever had the people from the academy and Christie's look at it. That would explain how they identified it as a fake."

"You mean because it was a fake," said Cate.

"Right."

"You think Farber and Laycutt were in on this together?"

"Yes."

Cate brushed a bright strand of hair away from her forehead.

"That's hard to believe," she said. "Harold's on the board of the museum. He's a major benefactor of the arts."

"But he's a collector, too," said Jamie. "Maybe he's always aspired to owning an Eakins. It's not an opportunity that comes along every day."

"Nevertheless. And even if it's true, why would he buy the forgery back from Mrs. Addison later, after it was denounced?"

"So he could destroy it." Michael jumped in. "Then years later he has you look at the real painting, and it's determined to be genuine. You've got to hand it to the guy. That takes balls."

"How do you know all this, Jamie?" Cate had a skeptical look on her face, as if she still didn't want to believe that Farber was involved. "It's all a bit fantastic, isn't it?"

"I know it because I have a blackmail letter Major Devero sent Laycutt. It mentions what he calls his *facsimile* of *Rush Carving*. He knew they had done something dishonest with it. Laycutt was to have delivered seventy-five thousand dollars to Devero's house tonight. That was the blackmail deal. In turn, Devero, I suppose, would have kept quiet."

"You say *was* to have delivered," Michael said. "He didn't?"

"No," said Ramsgill. "Instead of the money, Laycutt delivered something else. A fatal wound to the back of Devero's skull. He's dead."

Cate looked over at her husband with horror in her eyes, as if Michael himself had killed Devero.

"Sorry, Cate," said Jamie.

"No, it's all right. It's just that . . . you think . . . ?"

"It wasn't Farber, if that's what you're worried about. The blackmail letter was to Laycutt. I don't know if Farber got one too."

"Jamie," said Michael, "I'll go back to my original question. What happened to you?"

Ramsgill took a long drink, then cradled his glass between his fingers. The alcohol was beginning to mask the pain in his face.

"I got to Devero's house just after he was killed. Laycutt was still there. He surprised me and did this with a briefcase. He got away, but I got the briefcase. It had the blackmail money in it."

"The seventy-five thousand?" said Michael.

"Actually only fifty thousand. I don't know what happened to the rest. I suppose he could have been planning to short Devero, though I don't see why, if he were going to kill him anyway. The way it looked to me, Devero's death was premeditated. He was hit from behind and there was no sign of a struggle."

"And the fifty thousand? Did the police get that?"

"I don't know," Ramsgill said. "I left before they got there."

Michael's gray eyes slowly surveyed his brother. It was a calculating look, weighed down by a furrowed brow.

"You didn't talk to them?"

"No. I heard sirens and I don't know . . . I just ran. Laycutt must have called them to frame me. If I'd stayed I'd be a suspect right now."

"I've got news for you, brother. You're going to be a suspect anyway." Michael walked over to Jamie, hovering over him as he had when they were boys. "Nobody leaves a crime scene unnoticed," he said. "Fingerprints, fibers, witnesses. Where's this house?"

"Like I said," Jamie said softly. "In Jim Thorpe."

Michael turned and walked back over to the bar. He poured himself a small amount of scotch and tipped the glass back. He turned to his brother.

"Jamie, this isn't like when we were kids throwing water balloons at cars. This is murder. You don't run away from murder. Besides, you probably have information that can help the police. Do you know what Laycutt was wearing, what kind of car he was driving?"

"Not what he was wearing," he said. "It was too dark. But I think he's driving an Acura."

"What else?"

"Nothing. I really didn't get a good look at him."

"And what about you? Did anybody see you?"

Ramsgill arched his eyebrows, and rolled his eyes back slightly. "Jamie?"

"Well, yeah, probably. A guy saw me as I was leaving. And a patrol car chased me."

For the first time, Elena's arms let go of Jamie. She tilted his chin up with her hand, making him look her in the eyes.

"A patrol car did what?" she said.

"Chased me. And it crashed."

Elena let go of his chin, giving him the dismissing look of a disappointed mother.

"Whose car were you driving?" said Michael.

"Tod Farr's. Laycutt's partner."

"And where's the car now?"

"A block from here."

Michael looked over to Elena, and then to his wife. He walked to the phone near the refrigerator. He dialed, then said, "Give me the number for the Philadelphia police. The roundhouse at Seventh and Race."

"What are you doing?" asked Jamie, as Michael began to punch in the number.

"I'm calling the police."

"What for?"

"So you can talk to them. Clear your name. I know people there. They can contact the Jim Thorpe police."

"Don't do that," said Jamie. He rose and strode over to his brother. He felt light-headed. He didn't know if it was the alcohol or his injuries.

"Hello," said Michael. "Yes, this is Michael Ramsgill with Simpson, Strauss, Kulper and Timberlake. Is Bob Gunterson in, please?"

"Put down the phone," Jamie said.

"He's not in until tomorrow? Okay. Who in the investigations unit is on duty tonight?"

"Put down the phone, Michael."

"Lieutenant Ortiz? All right, I'll speak with him. What? Michael

Ramsgill. I'm an attorney. Tell him I'm friends with Gunterson."

"Michael!" cried Jamie, as he grabbed the receiver. The two of them wrestled for it, ending in a stalemate, each with a fist around one end of the receiver.

A moment later someone saying hello could be heard coming faintly from the ear piece.

"Goddammit, Michael, hang up."

"I'm doing what's best," he said. "You're in trouble, but if you turn yourself in now, tell them what really happened, everything will be okay."

"I'm not one of your clients," Jamie said.

"I didn't say you were."

"And I'm sick of being treated like a little brother. This isn't thirty years ago."

Michael's eyes hardened into a crystalline stare, looking into Jamie's eyes for the first time in Jamie's memory. Jamie stared back, steeled by the liquor and the resolve to use force if he had to, to keep Michael from talking to the police. Again the voice on the phone said hello.

"Jamie," said Elena. She was visibly upset, her eyes wide, her mouth wrenched into a frown.

"Put it down, Michael," said Cate.

Michael looked at her, then at Elena, before slowly letting go of the receiver. Jamie took it and hung it up. A nervous silence filled the room, broken only by the tick of the case clock in the hall.

"Thank you," he said to Michael.

Jamie walked back to the stool, before turning to face his brother.

"Look," he said. "I know they're going to find evidence of my having been there tonight, Michael. But the way it is right now, they would have as much on me as they would on Laycutt. I was seen there, it's obvious I was in a fight with somebody, the money has my fingerprints on it. And as far as Laycutt and Farber go, I'm assuming like you that the forgery was destroyed a long time ago. Cate, you told us this morning that Mrs. Addison apparently had no records of even having bought the Eakins. Without a forgery or acquisition records for the real painting, there's no proof that they even had a motive."

"What about the letter?" said Michael.

Jamie retrieved the letter from the pocket of his jacket. He handed it to his brother, along with the envelope.

"This is a pretty strong motive, Jamie. The envelope's addressed to Laycutt, and the letter implies that he did something fraudulent."

"Then how do I explain that the letter's in my possession?" said Jamie. "With my fingerprints all over it. And what was I doing at Devero's house?"

"Yours weren't the only prints on the letter, Jamie," said Cate.

"How *did* you get the letter?" said Elena.

"Laycutt left it at his mountain house. And he dropped the envelope this morning, when he fled his office."

"So you were at Devero's house to try to stop a murder," said Cate. "Isn't that right?"

"Of course it's right."

"But Jamie's got a point," said Michael. "It doesn't look good. For all the police know, he was acting on Laycutt's behalf. I'd like to keep this, Jamie."

"Why?"

"For safekeeping. And I'd like to run it past a couple of people at the firm. In total confidence. We have lawyers who deal with this kind of thing all the time."

"Okay," said Jamie.

Michael poured himself a bit more Scotch, but instead of drinking it, he just swirled it around in the glass. He finally set the glass down.

"So, if you won't turn yourself in, what are you going to do?" he asked.

"I want to talk to Anne Holden, Mrs. Addison's niece, to see if I can find more out about how she came into the painting. And I want to talk to Farber."

Cate's eyes shot over to her husband. Farber's involvement obviously had her nervous.

"Do you think that's wise?" said Michael.

"What do you mean?"

"If Farber's really mixed up in this, then he's not going to accede to questioning lightly."

"That's a risk I'll have to take," said Jamie.

Michael stared at Cate for a moment, then said:

"Look. Why doesn't Cate call Farber in the morning. Set up an appointment with him at my office. The four of us. I'll have a stenographer sit in. He'll either talk or he won't. But it'll be safe there."

Jamie thought about it, then nodded. He looked over to Cate and smiled. She returned it with a bittersweet smile of her own.

"Okay," he said.

"But once you talk to him, and after you talk to Mrs. Addison's niece, that's it, Jamie. You go to the police. And I'm not just playing big brother, here. The longer you don't talk to them, the worse you look."

"Fine."

"One more thing," said Michael.

"What?"

"Where do you think Laycutt is now?"

"I don't know," said Jamie. "And frankly I don't care."

Nine

David Laycutt stood leaning forward, his massive hands spread out on the countertop. He had been in this position for a couple of minutes, his body as tense and motionless as a steel spandrel, his eyes fastened to the paper before him. The note had been placed obliquely across the counter, where he was sure to see it. It had been written hastily, but with the fine precision of an architect's block lettering. The paper was Laycutt's, plucked from the slightly faded yellow pad next to the phone. The writing was Jamie Ramsgill's.

Was that possible?

Jamie had been here tonight? This is spiraling out of control, Laycutt thought. First the letter from Major Devero. Then his plan of how to deal with Devero going awry. And now to realize that it was Jamie who had gone to Devero's, to try to stop the whole thing.

But what did Jamie have to do with this, with anything related to this? How had he gotten involved? Laycutt struggled with his tortured mind to reveal an answer. Then he remembered that Jamie was to have come to the office that afternoon for an interview, an afternoon which now seemed like such a long time ago. He must have met with Tod, thought Laycutt, and somehow Tod had sent him after me. And if he had been here this afternoon, then it must have been shortly after I had left the cabin. Then he had seen the box of ammunition on the counter. And on the floor of the living area, the letter . . . what?

Laycutt's body twitched, and he found himself walking into the living area. He instinctively dropped to a knee, then both knees, finally all fours.

It's not here, he realized. Goddammit, Jamie, this has nothing to do with you!

He dropped the rest of the way to the floor, his broad torso pressing out flat on the wood, his gaze looking under the sofa. He then shut his eyes tightly, as if he were a kid being stalked by an imaginary monster, as if closing his eyes would make it all go away. But it wouldn't go away, and he now realized that Farber and Devero were not the only ones to worry about. Jamie Ramsgill knew the truth, and he had the letter to prove it.

"Jamie, wake up."

Jamie Ramsgill felt a hand cupped at his shoulder, shaking him gently, but with insistence. He looked up to see Elena, hovering over him like a dream.

"What time is it?" he mumbled. It was dark in their room, and he felt as though he had just dropped off to sleep.

"It's five A.M.," she said.

"Then why are you . . . ?"

"There's a phone call for you. In Cate's study."

Ramsgill's eyes flashed fear before he rolled out of bed and struggled to find the floor. His face felt twice its normal size, and his shoulder now ached like hell. He stumbled down the hall to a second-floor study Cate kept in the front of the house.

"Hello?" he said, holding the receiver a couple of inches from his ear.

"Jamie? This is Tod Farr."

"Yeah, Tod. What's up?"

"Can you come to the office?"

"Now?"

"Yeah."

"Why?"

"Can you come?"

"But why?"

"I'll tell you when you get here."

"But Tod—"

"Come on, Jamie, quickly."

Farr hung up.

Ramsgill lowered the receiver. He looked out into the darkness. He thought for a moment of calling Farr back, to tell him he was too tired to come. But there was an urgency to Farr's voice that was unmistakable. He returned to the bedroom to find Elena asleep again, her lithe legs draped over the side of the bed. He swung them back up onto the mattress and covered them. He then dressed quickly and let himself out by the front door.

He stepped out onto Michael and Cate's marble stoop, its top, like the tops of each of the three marble steps, concave from two centuries of wear. The rain had stopped but the air was still cool, and a night breeze whipped down Fifth Street. The granite cobblestones of the street were wet, glistening under the light glow of the street lamps. To his left, it was dark all the way up to Independence National Historical Park. To his right, heading off towards South Philadelphia, the street was interrupted only by a succession of traffic lights, set to flash yellow because of the early hour of the morning.

It took him five minutes of wandering to find where Elena had parked the Volvo, and another ten minutes to get across town. He realized that he should have returned Farr's car to him, but he didn't want to chance getting stopped. He parked just off Rittenhouse Square, where there was little activity save a few passing cars and an early morning newsman setting up his stand at the corner of Eighteenth and Walnut.

He was buzzed in, and when Ramsgill exited the elevator at the second floor, he found Farr slouched behind the reception desk. The office was empty and dark, cavernous in the absence of light. Farr was wearing a gold T-shirt and blue V-neck sweater. His hair was mussed and it didn't look like he had had much sleep.

"Thanks for coming," he said.

Ramsgill followed him halfway down the loft to a glass-enclosed office slipped under the mezzanine on the right-hand side. Farr switched on an Italian halogen desk lamp and sat behind his desk. Ramsgill took the chair opposite him. The walls of Farr's office were covered with framed black and white photographs of Laycutt/Farr buildings and awards the firm had won over the years. The photographs were as bold as the harsh chiaroscuro formed on Farr's face by the lamp, a face which Ramsgill took the opportunity to study.

Tod Farr must have been close to Ramsgill's age. He had wavy dark hair and a pleasant face, the hair worn long in the back. The square shape of his jaw was reinforced by rectangular wire-frame glasses, and the jaw was peppered with the black stubble of whiskers. His mouth was straight, as was his nose. The lamp light reflected off the lenses of the glasses, making it hard to see his eyes.

"I got a call from the police," Farr started slowly. "About a half hour ago."

"They traced your car?" said Ramsgill.

"I don't know. I don't answer the phone in the middle of the night. But they left a message on my machine saying that they wanted to talk to me. I'm thrilled. What's this about my car?"

Ramsgill recounted his story about going to Devero's, and about everything that had happened after that. When he had finished, Farr leaned back away from the light and clasped his hands behind his head.

"Fucking great," he said. "So they're probably at my house right now. Which means it won't be long until they come here. Where's the car?"

"In Society Hill. Near my brother's house."

"Where's David?"

"I don't know," said Ramsgill. He pointed to his face. "We met, he did this, he ran."

"And he killed Devero?"

Ramsgill nodded.

"But he's all right?"

"As far as I know."

"What happened to the money?"

"It's at Devero's house. I left it."

"I need that money, Jamie. We've already overextended our line of credit this month."

"The police might not find it."

"And David might walk through that door at any minute. But I wouldn't bet on it. I'd bet on the cops getting here first."

Ramsgill realized he should leave. He sighed.

"Sorry," Farr continued. "I guess it's my fault for not bringing the police in from the beginning."

"I know why David's being blackmailed," Ramsgill said.

Ramsgill told him about the blackmail note and about Mrs. Addison and her painting.

Farr looked down at his hands, then said softly, in the voice of a kid admitting a lie, "Jamie, I've been thinking about our conversation earlier today. When you called me from the road."

"Yeah?"

"I guess I have to believe what you're telling me about David. It's damn bizarre but after we hung up I remembered something about Mrs. Addison and David, something I hadn't thought about in a long time. Back then it really didn't mean shit to me. But now . . ."

"What is it?"

"When we were almost finished with the Addison's renovation, after Brook Addison had died, I got a call one day from Mrs. Addison. She was very upset, and from talking to David later, she was probably drunk. She threatened me. Or I should say, she threatened the firm. She told me that our work was deficient, that she wasn't going to pay her bills, and that furthermore, she was contemplating a lawsuit against us."

"How'd you respond?"

"At first I apologized, as she had definitely caught me off guard. As I told you, it was David's job. I really had no idea whether there was anything to what she was saying, or whether she was off her rocker. So I talked to David about it. He assured me that she was nuts, and that she had absolutely no basis for either a lawsuit or to not pay our fees. But I brought up the fact that even if there were no basis to it, we might consider making some kind of settlement offer to her. After all, if we pursued a claim against her, we were definitely going to incur legal costs."

"What was his reaction?"

"That I shouldn't worry about it. She'd pay her bills, he told me, and sure enough he was right. She eventually did. I later asked him how he knew she would pay, and he just said that she had a few skeletons rattling around in her closet. I didn't ask him about it at the time, and I'd have to say that that was the one time during our entire relationship together that I felt odd about David. I got the sense that he had actually threatened her somehow, and that he enjoyed it. It was damn weird."

"You mean that he threatened her physically?"

"No. More like he had some information about her that he could use."

Ramsgill thought back to something he had not been able to understand. Which was why, if Mrs. Addison knew that David had

88

switched her painting for a forgery, she had never come forward. If the Eakins painting had indeed been switched by Laycutt, and if she had realized it, she would have raised hell. Then there was what Cate had told him, that supposedly there were no records of Mrs. Addison even having bought the painting in the first place.

He glanced down at his watch. It was almost six. Three hours until his appointment with Anne Holden.

"I'm going to speak with Mrs. Addison's niece this morning," Ramsgill said. "Maybe she can shed some light on that."

Farr sat back again.

"You know, Jamie, I'm torn here. If David did kill Devero, then I might as well kiss the firm good-bye. Twenty years of busting my balls for nothing. So part of me wants to hush it up. On the other hand, if he did it, I can't sit by idle. A man's dead. David . . . "

"So, you're going to talk to the police?" said Ramsgill.

"I have to."

"And do you want me to talk too? After all, I'm the one who was driving your car."

"Do what you want," said Farr. "You can either stay and talk or leave. If you leave, I'll have to tell them that it was you who was driving it. To protect myself."

Ramsgill nodded.

"Fair enough," he said. "Do what you have to do. And I'm going to leave. Either way this should all come to a head in a few hours."

Ramsgill rose.

"Thanks, Tod. I'll be in touch."

Ramsgill left Laycutt/Farr Architects, now edgy, wary of the police and of Laycutt, anxious to talk to Harold Farber and to Mrs. Addison's niece. The sooner he got this over with, the better. He drove out to the Main Line, the string of affluent old suburbs west of the city. He had the address for Mrs. Addison's house, now owned by her niece, Anne Holden. He had decided that he couldn't wait until nine o'clock to meet Holden at her shop, and he hoped that she would see him at such an early hour. He was somewhat apprehensive, as she seemed to have been of two minds the day before.

The house was in Bryn Mawr, at the edge of the Mill Creek watershed. It was an area that could just as easily have been far away from the city, as the land surrounding the watershed was thick with woods and thin with development, most of the houses dating from at least the last century. Mrs. Addison's house was situated on a crook of land made by the sharp bend in a small stream. It faced the confluence of two old country roads and, along with three other houses, it was set close to the roadbed. The house was a large, two-story stucco, and though slightly flamboyant in its Victorian decoration, it had the simple proportions of an eighteenth-century structure.

Ramsgill parked and made his way down a slate path bordered by fiddlehead ferns rising up like a mass of charmed cobras. The grounds were verdant and well tended, with giant hemlocks hovering over the house like benevolent protectors. Surrounding him, the chorus of early morning song birds filled the air. At a French door on one end of a glassed-in rear porch, he picked up the morning paper and rang the bell.

A few minutes later he heard muffled sounds from within the house. A figure approached.

Through the beveled glass Ramsgill could see a face that was pretty in a haunting sort of way. It was pale-skinned and waiflike, with green eyes that were set close together. Above the eyes, black eyebrows looked as though they had been painted on by a calligrapher's brush. The mouth was pert and the chin acute, though hemmed in by the loose skin of middle age. Thick black hair flecked with gray was pulled backward into a bun.

Anne Holden became skeptical at the sight of Ramsgill and she froze at the door.

What do you want? she mouthed through the glass.

"Ms. Holden," he said in a high-pitched voice. "I'm Jamie Ramsgill."

She seemed to recognize the name, but she was nervous and he couldn't tell what she was going to do.

"I'm sorry to show up like this," he said, speaking slowly and loudly, as if she were deaf. "But if you could please see me for just a few minutes. It's important. Please?"

She hesitated for a moment, looking back into the main part of the house. She then winced, looking frustrated, as if she couldn't make up her mind. Finally, she unlocked the door and slowly pulled it open. Ramsgill paused, until she stepped out of his way. He moved forward and found himself in a small glassy anteroom with a brick floor, its perimeter lined with windows and houseplants. A corner fireplace was flanked by two Windsor chairs, and a cooking kettle hung from an iron rod suspended within the hearth. The ceiling of the room could not have been more than seven feet high, and hand-hewn beams made it feel lower still. The room smelled of old wood and moldy earth.

He reached out his hand.

"Jamie Ramsgill," he said, shaking fingers as long and cool as the deep burgundy sarong that Anne Holden wore.

"Please," he said again. "Just five minutes."

He handed her the newspaper.

"Let's go in here," she said flatly. "I'd offer you coffee but I don't drink it. Tea?"

"No thanks."

She led him up a couple of stone steps to the main part of the house. Ramsgill had the distinct sensation of stepping back into the past, into a house where things might be as they had been a decade ago, or perhaps even a century before. The floors of the house were uneven, and the wide plank boards squeaked with every step. Plaster walls were hung with neatly framed prints, and no wall was without a well-proportioned chair rail. The rooms were dim, and where lights burned at all it was from table lamps with dark shades, glowing like the faint stars of some faraway galaxy. Down the main hall and past a stair he followed her into a front parlor, all the while her looking back at him apprehensively. She sat businesslike in a Hepplewhite armchair. Ramsgill took a seat on an upholstered settee.

"What brings you here at such an hour, Mr. Ramsgill?" she said, lighting a cigarette and fanning out a match.

"I wanted to ask you about David Laycutt."

Anne Holden's head bobbed and she laughed softly, the laugh echoed by smoker's cough.

"Ah, David Laycutt," she huffed. "Ellie's favorite architect. You sit amongst the splendor of Mr. Laycutt's restorative talents."

Her sarcasm wasn't lost on Ramsgill.

"Your aunt didn't like Mr. Laycutt."

"No. She didn't. My uncle originally hired him. And when Brook died she felt used by him. Laycutt didn't take her seriously, he never listened to her."

"I heard it the other way around," said Ramsgill. "I heard she drank and that it was she who was inconsistent. That David bent over backwards for her to no avail."

"There might be some truth there. But I can tell you, her animosity was real."

"Did that animosity have anything to do with her Thomas Eakins painting?"

Holden's face signaled that Ramsgill had perhaps hit a nerve. She tugged on a big silver loop earring, then began to eye him more carefully, as if his presence suddenly had more meaning to her.

"Tell me, Ms. Holden. When did you first start working for your aunt and uncle?"

"Just after graduate school . . . 1975. I lived here when I first moved back to Philly, thinking that I'd eventually get my own place. Then Uncle Brook died, and I stayed on to help out Ellie. Last month, I inherited the house and the shop."

"So you were working for them when Mrs. Addison came into possession of the painting?"

"For her. My uncle had already died at that point."

"And that was also the time that Mr. Laycutt was working here?"

"It was."

"Did he have free reign of the house in order to do his work?"

"Of course."

"Was your aunt ever away during that period, for an extended period of time?"

Holden was staring at the floor. She thought for a second, then said, "The year after my uncle died we went to Europe for ten days. I thought it would be good for her. To get her mind off of his death. But . . . but . . . what are you getting at, Mr. Ramsgill?"

"I'm sorry?"

Anne Holden looked up. She drew down the cigarette and cast a fine plume of smoke up toward the ceiling.

"Why do you want to know about David Laycutt's reign of the house? And whether she was ever away?"

"Do you remember your aunt's reaction when she first had her Eakins painting looked at?" he said, ignoring her question. "By the man from the academy, and the other fellow?"

"Yes," said Anne Holden. "She was livid. She couldn't believe it was a fake."

"What did she do about it?"

"In all honesty, nothing."

"Did you think that was strange?"

"Yes. But I never said anything to her. I simply thought that she had been duped by the person who sold it to her, that for once in her life she had been taken."

"She was taken," said Ramsgill. "But not by the person she bought the painting from."

"Then by who?"

"David."

"I don't get it."

"David had a forgery made of the painting during the time he was working here. He swapped the fake for the real painting, perhaps when you were in Europe. He sold it to a man named Harold Farber."

"Farber? He's the one who bought the forgery, years later, when Ellie wanted to get rid of it."

"That's right. And he was in on it from the beginning. He bought the forgery from your aunt probably so he could destroy it. And now, there's hardly any way to prove what they did."

"Bastards," she said. "You're not kidding?"

"I wish I was."

"But what do you mean that you can't prove what they did. Who painted the forgery?"

"A man named Major Devero," said Ramsgill. "But he's dead. He recently sent David a blackmail letter. I went to his house last night to try to prevent David from killing him. Unfortunately I didn't make it in time."

"That's what happened to your face?"

Ramsgill nodded, then continued.

"I'm now trying to piece together what I can to prove that David set all this up, that he killed Devero. That's why I wanted to know more about how your aunt came to own the painting. Because I don't think she detested Laycutt for his work, but rather because she suspected him of having taken the painting. But she never went after him, and there's got to be a reason for that, just as there's got to be a reason she had no documentation on the painting. Cate says that you have no records?"

Holden shook her head. She was fingering the cigarette, rolling it between her thumb and forefinger.

"None that I know of," she said.

"But you were around when she acquired the painting."

"Sure, but that doesn't mean I know anything. All I know is that she bought the painting up in the Fairmount area of the city. As I understand it she literally stumbled across it. You know, Eakins himself lived up there, at Seventeenth and Mount Vernon."

"You don't have a name of the person she bought it from, an address, anything?"

"No."

"Did your aunt ever do business up there, buy antiques from anyone?"

"Not that I can recall."

Ramsgill exhaled, as much whistle as breath.

"You don't have anything she left? Papers, photographs, receipts?"

Holden began shaking her head before actually thinking it through. She then stopped, pulling her lower lip in and glancing upward.

"Wait a minute," she said, "I do have something." She rose and left the room. A few minutes later she returned with two Polaroid photographs, handing them to Ramsgill.

"I'd almost forgotten about these," she said. "But I don't see how they could help. Ellie took them the first time she went to see the painting."

Ramsgill took the pictures. They were essentially the same shot at slightly different angles, showing the lost version of Eakins' *Rush Carving*, photographed in an interior space. The framed canvas rested on a wooden floor and leaned against a column. The painting took up most of each photograph, but there were clues as to context. Ramsgill could see that the floor was made of narrow boards, probably maple, the kind used in old warehouses. The boards were set in the alternating diagonal pattern known as herringbone. And the column was a thin, somewhat rusted cast-iron column, which if the space were an industrial space of some sort, would have dated the building to the latter part of the nineteenth century. He knew that cast iron as a structural material had not really come to fore in America until the second half of the nineteenth century, and that it had been all but replaced by concrete within fifty years. And there was another clue, hardly visible, but distinguishable nevertheless. On the floor some distance beyond the painting was the oblique outline of a window, a cast pattern of light on the otherwise shadowed wood. From the light impression, Ramsgill could see that the window had an arched top to it and he could make out individual glass lites. The pattern was known as four over four, meaning that it was a double-hung sash with four glass divisions in the upper sash and four in the lower. The arched section was glass too, divided into two panes.

"Where'd you say these were taken?" he said.

"Ellie took them *in situ*, supposedly at the place where the Eakins' painting was found. I don't know, it looks like an old building, right?"

"It's a factory building," said Ramsgill. "Or a warehouse. From the later part of the nineteenth century. And if the pattern of light on the floor reflects a window on the building's facade, it might be possible to find it."

"Fairmount's a large neighborhood," said Anne Holden.

"But if I recall," said Ramsgill, "it's mostly residential. There are some old industrial buildings on the western edge and some up near Girard Avenue, but other than that . . . "

"It's a start," she said.

He looked at her, and a smile grew on his tired face.

"Unfortunately I need a finish. Could I borrow these?"

"Well, I don't think . . . "

"I'll return them, I promise. If we have any hope of proving what happened . . . "

"Take them," she said.

"I've got another question for you," said Ramsgill. "You said you thought that your aunt didn't do anything about the painting because you thought she had bought a fake. But David's partner intimated to me that David knew something about your aunt. I don't want to be insensitive, but it was something from her past. Something maybe she was embarrassed about, or wanted to cover up. Does anything like that come to mind?"

Anne Holden lit a second cigarette.

"No," she said.

"You don't sound too enthusiastic."

"Don't misunderstand me, Mr. Ramsgill, it's just that I don't know that much about her. I'm related to Brook's side of the family. My mother was his sister."

"I see. What was Mrs. Addison's maiden name?"

Holden took a drag on her cigarette as her brow scrunched up.

"Geez . . . I don't even remember. That's pretty pathetic, given that I'm her sole heir."

She rose and walked to a Pennsylvania German dower chest on the other side of the room, the fabric of her sarong clinging like a second skin to a shapely frame. She pulled out what looked to be an old album before returning to her chair. She placed the album on a coffee table, then began to go through it. Ramsgill found himself studying her profile.

"Here it is," she said. Holden slid the album across so Ramsgill could see and he tried to disguise the fact that he was staring at her. It was a wedding album, turned to a page with the wedding invitation glued to it. The invitation was from 1931. Mrs. Grace Beecham requests the pleasure of your company to the marriage of her daughter Elinor to Brook Addison of Wynnewood, Pennsylvania. The wedding was held at Bryn Mawr Presbyterian Church with a reception at the Merion Cricket Club in Haverford, Pennsylvania.

"So her maiden name was Beecham?" said Ramsgill.

"Yes."

"But it says here Mrs. Beecham. That would have been your aunt's mother. What about her father?"

"As I recall her father died the year Ellie was born. We're talking 1907 or something. Some kind of sailing accident in Newport. By the time I came along there was just Elinor."

"They were Newport people?" said Ramsgill. He was well aware that many of Philadelphia's better families summered in Newport, at least back in those days.

"I don't know," said Holden. "But I know she was from good stock. Her mother never remarried, though she lived quite comfortably until the mid-fifties on an annuity from her husband's estate. And besides, I'm sure Uncle Brook would have never been able to marry her otherwise. You see my grandparents, well let's just say that they were proper Philadelphia bluebloods. They were very conscious of class and the city's pecking order."

"If they married at Bryn Mawr Presbyterian, they must have been," said Ramsgill. "So Mrs. Addison was a Beecham. You say that's an old family too?"

Holden shrugged.

"I suppose. But again, there was only Aunt Ellie from the family that we ever knew."

Ramsgill was only half listening. He had been thumbing through the wedding album as he was talking and had come to a picture of the wedding party, standing on a porch filled with bouquets of flowers. Brook Addison was dressed in a morning suit, tall and handsome, a younger version of his father, who wore a military uniform of some sort. The elder Addison stood slightly behind his wife who wore a string of pearls the length of the Panama Canal. Elinor Beecham Addison stood next to Brook, a petite version of the widow Beecham, who flanked her on the right. Mrs. Beecham was a striking woman, who at the time of the photograph could have been no more than forty, very young, it seemed, to have a daughter old enough to marry.

Ramsgill then thumbed through a few more pages before returning the album to the box.

"This has been helpful," he said. "And thanks for seeing me."

He rose, as did Anne Holden. He followed her out to the rear room again, and to the door. He couldn't help but admire her stride, which synchronized with the sound of her dress chafing against her white-stockinged calves.

"Let me turn the tables here and ask you a question," she said, turning abruptly to Ramsgill as they stood on the porch. She looked around her. "I'm very fortunate to have all this now, to have inherited it. And the shop, of course. But you've gotten me thinking."

"About what?" said Ramsgill.

"About the painting. The fact that the painting Ellie bought *was* the real thing. That is, before Laycutt and Farber swindled her."

"That's right."

"What would a . . . do you have any idea . . . what a painting like that would be worth today?"

Ramsgill brushed a lock of hair away from his eyes.

"Cate says something like six, maybe seven million. And Farber's considering selling it."

Holden shook her head, squeezing her eyes shut as if she had the worst migraine.

"It would have been mine," she said.

Ramsgill nodded.

"I want it back," she said. "Do you understand?"

Ramsgill lightly touched the back of her hand, what was meant to be a comforting gesture, but one that gave him pause. Her hand was cold and her eyes stoic, yet he suspected that inside she was boiling. He hurried up the path to his car, brushing aside the morning mist, trying to comprehend how she must have felt.

Ten

It was eight forty by the time Ramsgill got back to Center City. The cloud cover had been pushed out by a cool front from the west, and a bright azure dome cradled the skyline. He exited the Schuylkill at Spring Garden Street and turned left, winding his way past the art museum. He had tried to call Cate on the way, but it seemed that both she and Michael, as well as Elena, were en route to work. He figured he'd see what he could find in the way of warehouse facades in Fairmount, then stop by Cate's office at the museum afterward to see if she had set up the meeting with Farber.

The Fairmount section of the city was a hilly area, just north of the museum and the Benjamin Franklin Parkway. With Anne Holden's photographs perched on his dashboard, Ramsgill began by making east/west traverses of the named streets, each successive street one way in the opposite direction of its predecessor.

The area closest to the parkway was a leafy urban village. He drove past Victorian brownstones, upscale townhouses, a couple of gray stone churches, and several bars and cafes. The people on the street here were young and well dressed, most of them with a lilt to their step. Further north the neighborhood became less urbane, with row after row of attached two-story brick houses, worker housing from the early part of the century. It was the kind of neighborhood where residents sit out on the sidewalk in folding lawn chairs. Mostly it was older people, but even here a few of the houses stood out as having been improved by the young professional crowd.

He finished the east/west trek without finding what he was looking for. He then began to drive the north/south streets, still encountering mostly residences. There were a few old commercial lofts up near Fairmount Avenue, huddled in the shadows of the Leviathan Eastern State Penitentiary. And some more all the way up at Girard. It wasn't until he made his way to the far western edge of Fairmount, however, out near Thirtieth Street, that there was a consistent mix of commercial architecture. At Twenty-eighth and Parrish he came across a brick brewery that had been converted into condominiums. And then an iron works from perhaps the 1890s that had been restored for a similar purpose. And another condominium called The Cooperage. But each of these buildings was large, and though from the same period as the one in Anne Holden's photographs, none of them had the four over four window with the distinctive arched top.

He was about to give up his hunt, when almost by accident, he made a right hand turn onto a tiny one-way street. The street was a single block long, and at its end was a T intersection with another small street, also one way. The second street headed south and was really no more than a cartway, paved in granite cobblestones, and flanked by small dark houses. But part way down on the left was a warehouse, the width of three houses, with a pair of large battened doors on the ground floor. It was made of old redbrick with corbeled band courses, and its second floor was fronted by a single tall arched window, over which was a suspended block and tackle. The glass pattern of the window matched that of the window in the photographs. It looked as though the window had at one time been used for moving goods in and out of the second floor. But if that were the case, then Ramsgill doubted that it would have been a double-hung sash. In fact, at an earlier time, it might not have been a window at all, but rather a door. The sash was freshly painted and the glass was modern float glass, with none of the waviness of nineteenth-century glazing.

As he approached the building Ramsgill could see that the window, like several other components on the building's facade, had been restored. And it was clear from the window boxes and terra-cotta planters flanking the batten doors, that the building was now a residence.

Ramsgill braked in the middle of the cartway and hopped out of his car. A moment later he saw the face of a child, pressed wide-eyed up against a closed iron gate that fronted a brick path on the left side of the building. It was a boy of four or five, with red hair and sharp blue eyes, engulfed by an oversized tie-dyed T-shirt. Quickly, an attractive woman came out a side door to the building and scurried up behind the boy.

Ramsgill smiled, trying to disarm the woman.

"I was just admiring your house," he said.

She nodded, but true to urban protocol, she stopped there, saying nothing else.

Ramsgill walked over to the gate, pulling a wallet from the back pocket of his chinos. He handed the woman a business card through the iron.

"I teach at Princeton," he said. "And I have an interest in old industrial architecture. This is a terrific building."

The boy looked up to his mother as she read the card.

"I suppose it is," she said.

"It looks as though it was a warehouse or something," he said.

The woman self-consciously wiped her mouth, unsure of whether to further the conversation.

"I think . . . it was a storage building for a soap company," she said reluctantly. "At least originally it was."

Ramsgill nodded. "I wonder," he continued. "Is the interior divided by columns? I figure the building's what, thirty-five feet across? Most structures this size and age had a single line of columns down the center."

"That's right," she said, now drawn into his questions.

"Cast iron?" he said.

She nodded.

"I've also seen some interesting floors in these old buildings. What are they, plank pine?"

"No . . . they're maple, I think. Is that possible?"

"Oh sure," said Ramsgill. "Then they're narrow."

"Yes."

"I thought so. Maple was fairly common, too. I recently looked at a loft near Broad Street that had a wonderful herringbone pattern to the wood floor."

"Really?" she said smiling. Her eyes had become open and friendly. "So does ours."

So far, so good, thought Ramsgill. But since he had lied to the woman about why he was interested in the building in the first place, how did he now leap to the discovery of the Eakins painting here?

"Did you restore the building?" he asked.

"No," said the woman, now perfectly at ease. "We bought it twenty years ago, already restored, back when my husband and I were first married. That was before gentrification up here. We just fell in love with the space, and it was what we could afford."

"It must have been a good investment."

"Oh yeah."

"If you don't mind my asking, who'd you buy it from?"

"A realtor named Phil Matzkin. He's fixed up a number of these places in the neighborhood. In fact, he did The Cooperage. But back then he was small."

"Matzkin? I don't believe I know that name. Where's his office?"

"Down on Pennsylvania Avenue," she said. "If you're really interested in the building you should talk to Phil. He's sort of a history buff."

The woman's son was now tugging at her skirt, obviously tired of listening to the conversation between her and Ramsgill. She gave him an admonishing look.

"I'll let you go," said Ramsgill. "And I will look up Mr. Matzkin."

The woman nodded and smiled, then scooped up the boy into her arms, mildly scolding him for interrupting the conversation. The boy grinned sardonically at Ramsgill as he was carried away like a sack of potatoes. Out of view of the mother, Ramsgill winked at him and got back into the car.

The Philadelphia Museum of Art is tethered to one end of the Benjamin Franklin Parkway, the other end of the Baroque axis stayed by City Hall. The two buildings could hardly be more different. City Hall is a great Victorian Merlin of cool gray granite, a second-Empire hulk with a clock tower the equivalent of a forty-story building. The art museum, in contrast, is a Greek god, spreading out horizontally on a tableau of sandstone, a mini Acropolis conceived by Julian Abele, the first black architecture graduate of the University of Pennsylvania and lead designer for the project in the office of Horace Trumbauer. It was a grand undertaking in 1920, a U-shaped edifice of over a half million square feet, replete with frieze sculptures of polychrome terra-cotta, and Corinthian columns of warm Kasota stone that rise like Saturn V rockets from a plaza four hundred feet wide. When funds to complete the museum originally fell short, it was suggested by the museum's director that they build only the two flanking wings on the presumption that Philadelphians would not leave the job unfinished. He was right, the center section was built, and the building today is a testament to the will of a city.

Ramsgill parked in the lot behind the museum and made his way to the rear doors. The museum was not yet open for the day, but the rear plaza was beginning to fill with school children and tourists, all milling around in the shadows of sculptures by Epstein and Nevelson. Ramsgill had stopped by the real estate office of Phil Matzkin, but Matzkin wasn't in. He left a message with Matzkin's secretary, saying that he would stop by again.

At the vestibule beneath the mammoth rear portico, Ramsgill was greeted by a uniformed guard. He inquired after Cate Chew, and a couple of minutes later Cate hurried across the stone of the rear foyer.

"Jamie, hi," she said. She signed for him to enter, and he followed her around to a suite of offices on the museum's ground floor. Cate had a small, neatly furnished office devoid of windows, which was made up for by the fact that three oil paintings worth more than Ramsgill's house in Princeton hung on the walls.

"Where have you been?" she said. "We were worried."

"I left a note that I was going to Laycutt/Farr's office."

"I know. But we called and you weren't there."

"Then Tod Farr must have told you where I was."

"He didn't," she said. Cate's eyes were flickering like candles, and her hands couldn't keep still.

"What's the matter?" he said.

"Don't you know?"

"Know what?"

Cate swiveled in her desk chair to some things atop a low bookshelf behind her. She picked up a newspaper and slid it across her desk to Ramsgill. He took one look at the headline and his heart skipped like a stone on a pond.

He read on. "Doctor Harold Farber," the column began, "inventor of the Farber neck collar and longtime patron to the arts, was found dead in a parking garage near Pennsylvania Hospital yesterday." The article went on to state that Farber had been stabbed to death, at some time after three o'clock in the afternoon. He had performed two operations at the hospital earlier in the day, changed into a sweat suit, and was just at the door of his Jaguar when his assailant caught up with him. A canvas bag was found three blocks away, with his dress clothes and squash racquet inside. His wallet was missing. He had been stabbed once in the back and twice in the chest, and his hands and arms were slashed in numerous locations, presumably self-defensive wounds. The body had been rolled beneath the car.

"Oh man," Ramsgill wailed. "This is unbelievable."

He put down the paper. He felt helpless, like one of those dreams where you fall into an unending abyss.

"On the news this morning they reported that he never had a chance," said Cate. "They said his killer must have been waiting for him. The mayor's calling for stepped-up police patrols downtown."

"Why?" said Ramsgill.

"To curb this kind of violence. There are animals out there, Jamie."

"You don't actually think this was a robbery, do you?" said Ramsgill.

Cate's lips parted and her eyes told him that she didn't.

"This was premeditated murder, Cate. Too much of a coincidence. David knew that Farber was at the hospital. He was desperate to speak to him."

"But, Jamie, that's horrible."

"Any worse than killing Devero?" Ramsgill said.

Cate conceded no with a shake of her head.

"I came by here to see if you had set up the meeting with Farber," said Ramsgill. He shrugged. "Now what the hell do I do?"

"Why don't you call Michael, Jamie?"

"Why?"

"After he heard about Farber he called the fellow he knows in the detective division at the police. He told him about what happened with you last night at Devero's."

"What?"

Ramsgill popped his hands down on Cate's desk and gave her an incredulous look.

"He promised," Ramsgill said. "Goddammit, Cate."

"Jamie, look, I agreed with you last night, but this is different. You can't talk to Farber now, and if what I'm hearing is correct, and you think David Laycutt did this, then you might be in danger."

Ramsgill breathed in deep and heavy. He had started this to help a friend, but now, it was apparent that his friend was a monster. He had two choices of the Hobson variety. Throw himself to the mercy of Michael's acquaintances at the police, or stay out and have his one-time housemate catch up to him with a knife.

"This is absolutely unbelievable," he said again.

The phone on Cate's desk rang softly, and she picked it up.

"Hello," she said.

She listened silently before speaking again.

"Thanks for returning my call, Vibeke. I just wanted to offer Claudia my condolences. I'm so very sorry. No. That's not important now. My brother-in-law wanted to speak to Dr. Farber about something. Really, it's not important. Okay, give Claudia my love, and let her know that everyone here at the museum is thinking about her."

She hung up.

"Who was that?" asked Ramsgill.

"That was Harold's secretary," said Cate. "Vibeke Lidz."

"And who's Claudia?" said Ramsgill.

"Farber's wife."

Ramsgill's eyes widened, imploring a question.

"What?" said Cate. "You want to speak to her?"

Ramsgill shrugged.

"Leave her alone, Jamie. Give her some peace."

Ramsgill nodded, but it was a half-hearted nod.

"I went to see Anne Holden this morning," he said. "And I've found out something about the painting's provenance."

"You have?"

"Yes. I think I located the building where the painting was found. Just north of here. It's an old warehouse."

"How'd you do that?"

Ramsgill reached into his shirt pocket and pulled out the two Polaroids.

"You were right," he said. "Anne Holden had no records. But she did have these."

He handed them to her.

"I'm going to see the real estate agent who renovated the building about the time Mrs. Addison bought the painting. I'm thinking that she bought it from him."

"Oh?"

"By the way," said Ramsgill. "Did you know that Mrs. Addison was a Beecham?"

"A what?"

"Her maiden name. It was Beecham. Her mother was named Grace Beecham."

"So?"

Ramsgill shrugged.

"I don't know, I thought you might know the family name. Anne Holden said that they were wired into local society."

Cate shook her head slowly.

"Doesn't ring a bell," she said.

Ramsgill took the pictures back from Cate. He then started to ask another question, but given that Michael had contacted the police already, he realized that if he were going to avoid being picked up that he probably couldn't trust Cate.

He rose, deciding to leave instead.

"Well, I'd better be going."

"Where to?" she said.

"My lips are sealed," he said.

Cate thought for a moment, then said: "You're going to Farber's, right? To speak to Claudia."

Ramsgill didn't answer.

"You've got to tell me where you are going, Jamie."

"Why? So you can tell Michael? So he can phone the police?"

"Jamie, don't be silly. He's doing this for your protection."

Ramsgill stared at her, trying not to take out his animosity toward his brother on her.

"Is he really? Or does he just want to handle it his way. The way he did with Dad, never mind what I think. I can't believe he . . . "

He paused, biting his lip. Cate realized that it was futile to try to make him understand, and that he wasn't going to give her any information.

"Be careful," she said.

Ramsgill turned and walked away.

The bell above the door chimed as Ramsgill entered the offices of Matzkin Properties, a homey suite of rooms on the ground floor of a Victorian brownstone. Ramsgill asked for Phil Matzkin and was told to take a seat. He shuffled through old copies of *Investors' Daily* and the *Urban Land Institute Journal,* before he was shown back to a paneled office in the middle of the building, what looked to be an old library.

There he was met by a bearded man with streaked gray hair, pulled back into a ponytail. The man wore pressed blue jeans and a starched pink shirt, the front of which hung well over his waistline. His face held the scars of adolescent acne, but his smile was wide and his hazel eyes vibrant.

"Phil Matzkin," he said cheerfully, his head shaking in rhythm with his pumping hand. "Have a seat."

Ramsgill slipped into a chair of worn green leather, noticing the sight and smell of books, most of them old, lining the shelves around the room.

"What can I do for you?" Matzkin said.

Ramsgill considered for a moment perpetuating his lie about an interest in industrial architecture, but he realized that unless he was straight with Matzkin, he'd probably never get from him what he wanted.

Instead, he reached into his pocket and tossed Anne Holden's polaroids across the desk.

"Do these look familiar to you?" he said.

Matzkin's glasses hung from a silver chain around his neck, and he brought them up and rested them on his nose. He studied the photographs for a moment, then slipped the glasses off and looked across his desk at Ramsgill.

"Maybe," he said. "Why?"

"I stopped by the building where the pictures were taken today," Ramsgill said. "And I spoke to the owner. I didn't get her name, but she told me that she and her husband had bought the building from you back in the seventies, after you'd fixed it up."

"That's correct."

"And I got the photos from a woman named Anne Holden. She's the niece of Elinor Addison, the woman who took these pictures, also during the seventies."

"Okay."

"Mrs. Addison bought the painting in the photographs at about this time, presumably from the person who owned the building. What I wanted to know is if that person was you."

"Can I ask *why* you want to know?"

"It's a long story, but suffice it to say that Mrs. Addison ultimately sold the painting, thinking it was worthless. But she was defrauded. My sister-in-law has examined the painting for the new owner and she thinks it's worth several million dollars."

Ramsgill watched as Matzkin's jaw began to move, as if it were sore and he was trying to loosen it up.

"You're saying this painting's worth several million dollars?"

"That's right."

"How many million?"

"Six, maybe seven."

Matzkin whistled through his teeth, the sound petering out like a bottle rocket fading into the distance.

"I'm a fool," he said.

"Why? Because you sold it to her?"

"Yeah." He laughed. "I thought at the time I was making a killing. She paid me two thousand dollars for it, cash. And that was twenty years ago."

"How did you two hook up?" Ramsgill asked.

"She searched me out," he said. "She seemed to know some people in the neighborhood, some of the old-timers. I guess she just put word out on the street, I really don't remember who made our introduction."

"What do you mean? She put the word out? She was looking for antiques?"

"No. She was looking for artwork. Victorian paintings. Specifically figure studies. You see, I bought that old place lock, stock, and barrel. It was a disaster inside. Cases of moldy soap, old machinery downstairs, junk furniture, piles of newspapers, tools, and so forth. We pulled stuff out of every cranny. Mixed in with all the crap on the second floor were a bunch of paintings. Most of them were molded or ripped, a lot of them had been painted over. But this one caught her eye."

"And she bought it on the spot?"

He laughed again, the laughter rounding out into his answer.

"Hell no. She took these pictures and went away for a day. Then she came back, acting like she wasn't really interested. But I could tell that she was, and that the only reason she had left was to get me to lower my price. I thought I was some sort of Rockefeller when I refused to budge on two thousand. But now . . . you say seven million dollars?"

Ramsgill nodded.

"Un-fucking-real," said Matzkin.

"Tell me, if you don't mind," said Ramsgill. "Who'd you buy the warehouse from? Before you renovated it?"

"From a fellow named Helm. Let's see . . . "

Matzkin had a little trouble working himself up out of his chair, his elbows all at angles as he pushed himself up. Ramsgill realized that Matzkin was older than he had at first thought. Matzkin limped over to a bookshelf on the other side of the office and ran his fingers over a series of blue notebooks that lined one of the shelves.

"Here we go."

He returned to the desk and plunked the notebook on top of it. Handwritten neatly in magic marker on the notebook cover was 721 N. PASCAL STREET, the address of the warehouse. He opened it and thumbed through it until he came to a copy of a deed.

"This is the deed," he said. "Before I bought it, of course. We got it in seventy-one. Sold it to the woman you spoke to in seventy-six, I think. Richard Helm owned it before that. And you can see, he only owned for eight years. Bought it from someone named Mulrooney. I know Helm's still around but he must be pretty old. I don't know who the hell Mulrooney is."

"Could I take a look at something?" Ramsgill asked.

Matzkin slid the book over to Ramsgill.

"I thought I saw . . . yeah, here . . . " Ramsgill flipped to the front of the notebook, where a pocket folder of photographs was located.

"Are these pictures of the building?"

"Oh yeah," said Matzkin. He fished out the lot and began shuffling through them, pitching them in Ramsgill's direction, offering commentary about each one. "Here's the front of the building before restoration. . . . It even shows where the block and tackle was broken off. . . . We rebuilt that, you know . . . and here's one of the old machines downstairs. . . . What was it? . . . A die-cutter of some sort . . . and here's the upstairs. . . . Shit, you can see all the junk . . . and . . . "

"Wait," Ramsgill said. "What's this?"

Ramsgill handed the photograph back to Matzkin.

"Oh, those things," said Matzkin. "Yeah, there were several of those. Some sort of wood carvings."

"They're ships' scrolls," said Ramsgill. "They're like the ones in the painting."

Matzkin leaned down to study one of the photographs.

"Huh," he grunted. "I never noticed that. And if Mrs. Addison did, she never let on to me."

"I wonder . . . " said Ramsgill.

"What?"

"I don't know. I just wonder whether the painting was made right there. In your building."

"I don't know," said Matzkin.

"You ever hear of Thomas Eakins?" said Ramsgill.

"Sure."

"He was the artist who painted the picture. My sister-in-law thinks that the model in the picture was Eakins' mistress. Eakins lived not far from Pascal Street. And there's no doubt he tried to hush up the existence of the painting."

"So you think their tête-à-tête took place in my building?"

"Could be. That would explain what all of those canvases were doing there. They could have been there for sixty or seventy years if no one was living there, and if the building was used only for storage. It would be interesting to know who owned the building back then."

"There are ways of finding out," said Matzkin.

"Yeah?"

"Sure. City Hall. Do a deed search."

"Can anybody do that?"

"Absolutely, if you have a little time. They have clerks there in the Office of Records who can help you. And the deed books go way back in time."

"Sounds like I need to get to City Hall."

"I think so."

"Well, look, Mr. Matzkin, thanks for your help."

Matzkin rose and stuck out his hand.

"My pleasure," he said, offering up a wry smile, the thought of a lost fortune implanted firmly in his mind.

Ramsgill pulled up to the grand iron gates of Pennwood House, without an appointment and with what he thought would be the slimmest of chances of actually speaking to Claudia Farber. He felt like a heel to even attempt it, given that she was less than twenty-four hours from learning of her husband's death, and that Ramsgill's own accusations would be like salt on a newly opened wound. But as he idled his car and tried to muster up the courage to use the intercom at the gate, circumstances decided for him that he would drive onto the property.

At that moment, a gray and burgundy Brinks truck exited the grounds, automatically tripping the gate sensors leaving the gate open. The truck pulled away, and Ramsgill started to turn in. As he did, he noticed a white van moving at high speed toward him. He just made the drive before the van passed within inches of his rear bumper. The gates closed behind him and he followed the long winding blacktop up to a parking area beneath the lacy shade of some honey locust trees. The parking area looked like the lot of an upscale car leasing company, filled with late-model Mercedes, BMWs, Lexuses, and Range Rovers, and ringed in granite Belgian block. Ramsgill felt self-conscious about parking his nine-year-old Volvo there, but he pulled into an empty space, then made his way by foot toward the house.

Pennwood House looked patently out of place on this stretch of the wide Delaware River, a waterway lined by marinas, warehouses, and container facilities. The house itself was fervently Greek Revival—muscular, white, and severe—most assuredly built on the banks of the river at a time long before the area had been developed. It was essentially a big box of a building, set beneath a single pedimented gable. The rear had no porch, but rather Doric pilasters two stories high that visually held up the pediment. Between the pilasters were triple-hung windows perhaps eight feet tall, shuttered with louvered shutters, pale green in color against the white of the house's walls.

As Ramsgill approached the entry he heard the hubbub of voices from the other side of the house. He took a small cinder path to the left of the house, arriving at the front lawn, which spread all the way down to the river. There a number of well-dressed people were milling about, friends and relatives, Ramsgill presumed. A uniformed man was making his way through the small crowd with a tray of fluted glasses of orange juice. Another servant, or caterer perhaps, had a tray of pastries. And yet another man, with nothing in his hands, spotted Ramsgill as he rounded the corner of the house. The man began to head in his direction. Ramsgill's body solidified, but he realized there was nothing he could do.

"Excuse me!" the man called, approaching rapidly.

"I, uh . . . " mumbled Ramsgill.

"Sir, if you don't mind, Mrs. Farber wanted each of the visitors to sign the guest book."

Ramsgill nodded, his shoulders loosening, his breath returning.

"And as I noticed that you had come around the side," continued the man, "I just wanted to make sure that you make your way into the house first. The register's in the front hall."

"I'll be sure to," Ramsgill said.

"Very well." The man disappeared back toward the crowd.

Ramsgill made his way across the lawn. The grounds of the house were large, and there was no sign of development in any direction, save for the view across the wide water to New Jersey. Sunlight painted the grass with impressionistic slivers of gray green, the shadows of old oaks. Big boxwoods shaped like dense cumulus clouds lined a path that tumbled down to the water. At the shore a freshly whitewashed boathouse had a large yacht moored beside it, the boat overwhelming the boathouse in size. Ramsgill turned his gaze to the front porch of the house. It was perhaps the closest thing he had ever seen in America to the *pronaos* of a Greek temple. It jutted forward like a breastplate of heraldic armor, fronted by a wide band of marble steps. Six massive fluted columns stood sentry to the porch, and the soffit was indented by deeply stepped coffers.

Ramsgill hopped the stairs to the porch. At the door he stepped aside to let two women in perfectly tailored suits and two hundred dollar haircuts pass. He then walked into the main hall of the house, a chamber the volume of a decent-sized basketball court. He spotted a table at the other end of the hall, next to the rear door. As he walked toward the table, he took in his surroundings. The floor of the hall was an alternating black and white patterned marble. Three exquisite neoclassical light pendants hung from the ceiling. The walls of the hall were lined with paintings, most of them pastoral scenes from an earlier century. Wide arched openings lead into flanking rooms, each decorated as if Sister Parrish herself had personally overseen them. An elliptical stair swept up to the second floor.

When he reached the table, he took up the pen and signed his name in the book. His eyes then traveled to an adjoining room, where three women and a man stood talking. The man wore a pinstripe suit, its cool gray material only slightly darker than his gray hair. He stood next to a thin woman whose silver hair was swept up into a beehive, a rococo contrast to the midnight blue skirt and blouse she was wearing. She had the deep bronze tan of a lifeguard.

Across from them was a middle-aged woman in a stiff light brown suit. She had a plain pale face and workaday haircut, and her presence evaporated in contrast to the woman who stood beside her. This last woman had a diminutive body and a youthful face that Ramsgill could only guess was Latin. She too was tanned, her skin a smooth golden brown set off by teeth the iridescent white of pearls. She had thick black hair swept over her shoulders and full lips with that little separation between them that high fashion models have, making them look as though they are forever whistling. She wore a loose black dress that hung low around her perfectly shaped shoulders and collarbone. Ramsgill immediately realized who she was. She was Claudia Farber, and she must be, he realized, forty years younger than her deceased husband.

The man in the suit and the lady in blue nodded to Mrs. Farber, then backed out of the room. It was then that Ramsgill saw the object around which the group had been standing, on a small easel in front of a fireplace. It was the Thomas Eakins painting, which must have just been delivered from Cate and Michael's by the armored car. Ramsgill swallowed, and realized he had lost any nerve he might have had to introduce himself. He could see that Mrs. Farber was distraught, her near lineless face nevertheless impressed with despair. He started to back away from the open doorway when she surprised him, disarming him with a polite smile. He stood uncomfortably for a moment, knowing that he had to enter the room. He approached her the way one would approach royalty, then held out his hand until it met the soft skin of her bejeweled fingers.

"Mrs. Farber," he said, somewhat haltingly. "My name is Jamie Ramsgill."

Claudia Farber's eyes darkened, as if she were seeing a familiar face to which she couldn't attach a name. In actuality, Ramsgill realized, it was the opposite. She knew the name Ramsgill, but knew he was not Cate Chew's husband.

The woman in the brown suit said, "This is Cate Chew's brother-in-law."

Ramsgill nodded and forced a smile.

"It's nice of you to come," said Claudia Farber. She spoke with an accent, and Ramsgill wondered if she were from South America.

"I'll be straight, Mrs. Farber. I can't claim to have come here to give my condolences, though I am sorry about your husband. Frankly, I'm in trouble, and you may be the only person who can help me."

"Mr. Ramsgill," said the woman in brown, whose own accent confirmed that she was Dr. Farber's secretary, Vibeke Lidz. "This is inappropriate. Now if you would like to leave, I'll see that Joseph escorts—"

Mrs. Farber broke in. "What kind of trouble, Mr. Ramsgill?" She was staring up at his face, studying his contusions.

The front door opened and Ramsgill turned to see an older couple approaching the guest register.

"Could we talk alone?" he said, turning to Mrs. Farber again. "It's about your husband. And about the painting."

Claudia Farber walked around Ramsgill to the opening leading into the hall. She was about to close the pocket doors when the couple in the hall recognized her. She said hello then excused herself, pulling the doors to. She returned to Ramsgill and Lidz and offered Ramsgill a seat near the fireplace. Lidz sat stiffly next to Claudia Farber.

"Like I said," Ramsgill started, "I was sorry to hear about your husband's death. I was shocked when Cate told me this morning. What I wanted to ask you was if you knew of any reason your husband might have been murdered."

Ramsgill watched Claudia Farber's reaction carefully. He had wondered what, if anything, she knew of the real story of the Eakins painting, and how it had come into her husband's possession. The puzzled look on her face lead him to believe that she knew nothing.

"The police said it was robbery," she replied.

"Do you believe that?" asked Ramsgill.

"Shouldn't I?"

"How well do you know David Laycutt?" Ramsgill said.

Her head tilted almost imperceptibly, before a hint of recognition washed across her face.

"The architect?"

"Yes. I know he was a friend of your husband's. Did you and your husband see him often?"

"No," she said casually. "We bump into him once in a while, at charity balls and galas. But we don't run in the same circles."

"Did your husband have any recent contact with Laycutt?"

Claudia Farber shook her head. "Not that I know of."

Vibeke Lidz's face contorted into a frown.

"Mr. Ramsgill, you know that David Laycutt called here yesterday. I told you that on the phone."

"I'm not saying you didn't. I just wondered if Mrs. Farber had known of any recent contact."

Farber again shook her head.

"How about a man named Devero?"

"Devero?"

"I know Mr. Devero," said Lidz. "He was a recipient of one of Harold's grants . . . years ago. I administer the program."

"That's right," said Ramsgill. "He received one of the very first fellowships. Along with Laycutt."

Vibeke Lidz's eyebrows arched before falling again. Claudia Farber looked at both Ramsgill and Lidz, then said, "Mr. Ramsgill, I don't want to be rude but I have guests. What's your point here?"

"My point is that I think it's very doubtful your husband was killed in a robbery. How much do you know about his Thomas Eakins painting?"

"Which one?" she said turning to the easel. "He has two."

Ramsgill had seen numerous paintings in the hall of the house, but none by Eakins.

"This one."

Claudia Farber smiled. She smoothed the hem of her skirt on her bare bronze thigh.

"I know that it's very beautiful," she said. "And erotic. And also worth a great deal of money, now that your sister-in-law has authenticated it."

"And do you know how your husband came to own it?"

She nodded.

"He bought it from an antique dealer," she said. "Before I knew him."

"Not exactly," said Ramsgill. "What he bought was a forgery."

"Not according to your sister-in-law."

"I'm afraid so. He already had the real painting, and he only bought the forgery so he could destroy it."

Claudia Farber gave Ramsgill a look like they were in a bar, and he had just bombed with a pickup line.

"What are you talking about, Mr. Ramsgill?"

Ramsgill stood and walked over to the painting. He looked at it for a brief second, then turned around to face the two women. He then laid it out plainly, sparing nothing about her husband's complicity in the crime. All the while he studied their faces, but neither of them betrayed any knowledge of what he was talking about, if they indeed possessed it.

"Mr. Devero was murdered last night," he said in summary, "just hours after your husband. There were only two people who could point a finger at David Laycutt. And now they're both dead."

"You are saying that Dr. Farber was involved in this plot?" said Lidz. "That's not possible. What proof do you have?"

"I think he paid for the forgery," said Ramsgill. "Laycutt didn't have that kind of money. It must have cost them several thousand dollars."

"No," Lidz protested. "I've kept Dr. Farber's financial records for more than twenty years. I would have known about such a payment."

"I have a letter that contradicts you, Ms. Lidz," said Ramsgill.

"If you're so certain about this," said Claudia Farber, "then why don't you go to the police?"

"I will. Soon. I was hoping you could help me, though. Your husband's dead now, there's nothing that can be done about that. You don't have anything to cover up."

Vibeke Lidz jumped up and cocked her head. It was an unkind thought, but she suddenly reminded Ramsgill of a chicken.

"I think Mr. Ramsgill should leave," she said. "Claudia?"

"Calm down, Vibeke. Mr. Ramsgill, we're not covering anything up. Don't you think I want to know the truth about my husband's murder?"

Ramsgill had already thought about that question. He considered his next statement carefully.

"Maybe," he said. "But maybe not."

Claudia Farber's wide brown eyes intensified their hold on Ramsgill.

"What are you implying?" she said.

"If your husband *was* murdered by Laycutt," he said, "then presumably it's because my story about the fraudulent painting is true. If it's true, then your husband came by his Eakins painting illegally. And you might lose the painting. So you see, it might be in your best interest to remain quiet."

Ramsgill sat back, waiting for the volcano to erupt. He had no idea whether he believed what he was saying, but if he was going to pry anything out of these two women, he was not going to do it by virtue of decorum.

Vibeke Lidz was still standing.

"There's just one deficiency with that theory," she said, taking up the mantle for Claudia Farber. "One simple problem."

"What?" said Ramsgill.

"The Eakins painting will not go to Claudia anyway."

Claudia Farber's eyes flicked upwards to the secretary. For the first time during their entire meeting, a grin, though a small one, was implanted on Lidz's pale cheeks.

"Dr. Farber signed a codicil to his will, just this week," she said. "It seems that your sister-in-law convinced him to leave the painting to the museum. So you see, Mr. Ramsgill, we're right back where we started. Any thoughts you might have had that Dr. Farber was mixed up in this have been wiped out by the stroke of a pen. They're false. Or certainly moot. So I would suggest that you leave now, as I am sure Claudia has people to greet. Or perhaps she'd like to be alone."

Lidz strutted to the pocket doors and flung them open.

Ramsgill turned to Claudia Farber, who looked as though she had just lost a child. It was clear that she knew nothing about the codicil. He rose slowly and nodded to her, then followed Lidz out of the room.

As he drove south back into the city Ramsgill reflected on Vibeke Lidz's revelation regarding the codicil to Farber's will. He felt as though he was climbing a Sisyphean hill. Not only had he failed to get evidence of Farber's involvement in the plot to acquire the Eakins painting, but the fact that Farber had decided to donate the painting to the museum had ripped a gaping hole in his theory of Farber and Laycutt's having conspired together to defraud Mrs. Addison in the first place. It wasn't that he believed Ms. Lidz's statement that she would have known about the payment to Devero, because if Farber had indeed paid for the forgery, then certainly he would have done so without her knowledge. She could also be lying, he knew that. What didn't hold together though, and what tore at his insides, was Farber's simply giving the painting away.

Where did that leave him, Ramsgill wondered. It was still possible that Farber and Laycutt *had* been together on the deal, but that maybe later Farber had had a change of heart. Perhaps his conscience brought him back to reality, or at least back to some ethical grounding. Or perhaps Devero had contacted him with a blackmail demand too. By donating the painting to the museum Farber would be casting suspicion away from himself, though he would still have to deal with Laycutt, who presumably would be losing his stake in the whole thing.

Is that why Laycutt had killed him? But how could Laycutt have even known about the will? Farber's own wife didn't know about it. And even if Laycutt did, what good would killing Farber do? It might satisfy a lust for revenge, but it wouldn't get Laycutt a share of proceeds from the sale of the painting. Any agreement between them to share the money would hardly have been made in the form of a contract.

Ramsgill paused midthought. He was now traveling on I-95, and there was a white van some fifty yards behind him in his lane. Was it following him? Was it possible that it was the same van he had seen at Claudia Farber's? The one that had almost hit him as he had turned into the property? He had been fearful ever since leaving Devero's last night, but his fear wasn't paranoia. He knew the difference. This vehicle *was* following him, and suddenly, swiftly, his insides seized up, and the blood began to pump a little harder in his veins.

He slowed to fifty and the van slowed too. A mile later he sped up, then decided to exit at Allegheny Avenue. His eyes didn't stray from the rearview mirror, and at first he thought that the van hadn't exited. But without warning it came out of nowhere, whipping around him—no, not really around him, more like bearing down on him in his own lane. Ramsgill swerved to his right, the car speeding along on the debris-strewn shoulder, and then when he looked in the driver's side mirror, he saw the van filling it and growing larger.

Suddenly his world went haywire. A deafening CRACK lit the air, penetrating Ramsgill's car, even though the windows were rolled up. Ramsgill's eyes had been trained on the van's reflection in the side mirror, and for a moment he thought that the van had exploded. But he realized it was the mirror itself that was gone, disappearing into a ball of spent energy. Everything seemed to go to angles then, flashes of light and shards of glass, tilting planes of metal. His car swerved again, this time wildly, swiping a concrete barrier. The van then roared past him, trying to cut him off as it did.

Ramsgill's mind stopped racing just long enough to realize what had happened. A gunshot had blown away the mirror, and it had come from the van. The van was at the bottom of the ramp now, turning right. Without thinking, Ramsgill gunned the engine and followed. The van sped on, too far ahead of him for Ramsgill to read the license plate, bouncing through a yellow light like a bucking bull. Ramsgill pursued as the light turned red. The van turned at the next side street. By the time Ramsgill had made the turn, the van was at the end of the block. It disappeared onto an avenue under the El, and Ramsgill slowed. What the hell was he going to do anyway? Politely ask the driver to replace his mirror?

He crept up to the intersection like a dog with its tail between its legs and put on the parking brake. He hopped out and took a look at the right side of his car. A long ugly scar ran through both doors.

"Shit," he said under his breath.

He took a look around him. The avenue under the El constituted another world, where daylight filtered down only in small increments. It was early afternoon, but already prostitutes were cruising up and down the glass-cluttered concrete median, their peacock-colored clothes doing nothing to perk up faces that had a hard time forcing smiles for passing cars. Young men leaned against graffiti-papered walls, drinking from paper bags or fanning money, popping their wads of bills with the backs of their hands, show time for passing motorists. A police car, its hubcaps missing, was parked halfway down the block in an abandoned lot among old mattresses and washing machines, the somber eyes of the officer inside cast downward to a clipboard of paperwork, oblivious to the scene around him.

Ramsgill got back into the car, wanting nothing to do with a cop. He started to find his way back to the expressway, but on second thought, he pulled a piece of paper from his pocket and changed course directions. A few blocks to the west he entered the part of the city known as the Badlands. When he reached Fifth Street, he slowed, turning north onto a block that looked like the aftermath of a blitzkrieg. To his right was a crumbling factory whose long brick frieze four stories above the street held the vestiges of a sign which read *Geis Brothers' Shoes*, so faint that it reminded Ramsgill of a Pompeian mural. In front of the factory three cars looked like they had been in a brawl. To his left, in the shadows of the factory, was a line of fifteen or twenty row houses, most of them boarded up. At the end of the street a small crowd gathered.

He searched the houses for signs of life. Midway up the block he saw a recognizable number on one of the few houses that looked to be occupied. He pulled up to the curb and got out of the car. Almost immediately he could see a couple of people break off from the crowd at the end of the block and make their way in his direction.

He climbed a stoop and knocked on a metal door through an iron security gate. Out of the corner of his eye he could see the two people approaching, one of them a man who was styling, the other a woman in a black leather shirt so short that Ramsgill wondered why she bothered to wear it at all. He knocked again, his nerves bundled up like bailing wire. He got no answer, but then to his left, from behind a curtain in a barred bay window, he saw the face of a little boy staring out at him. Then the curtain opened further, and a big black woman with short red hair and glasses gave him a look that could put the fear of God into Jeffrey Dahmer.

"Yo!"

Ramsgill turned to see the man and woman, who were much closer now, and he realized that the man was really a boy, perhaps fifteen, with dark ebony skin. He walked with a swagger and wore baggy white shorts that rode a few inches above the tops of his huge sneakers. His swinging arms were taut and muscular, and he had the neck of a tight end. The woman was Latino, and she was wearing a big brunette wig. Her tight knit top was emblazoned with glittered letters that read CHIC N' SASSY. Her legs looked like two bruised bananas.

"How 'bout it cuz?" said the kid, pausing as they reached Ramsgill, circling his car. "You the police? Naw I don't think so. I don't think so. What ya'll need? The Love Train. Darjeeling. Beam me up, Scotty?"

"Get the hell . . . out of here!"

The booming voice came so quick and hard that it almost knocked Ramsgill off the stoop. He stumbled backwards, slipping to the second step. He looked sheepishly up to the now-open door of the house from where the voice had come. The woman with the red hair filled the entire door frame behind the iron bars, but she was not looking at Ramsgill. Her eyes held the young man and woman in a vise grip, and Ramsgill turned to see the pair scampering off down the street. Someone from the crowd at the corner yelled something Ramsgill couldn't make out, then the entire crowd broke into laughter.

"Ms. Devero?" he said, once they were back at the end of the block.

She looked down at him like he was an insect, and she had half a mind to squish him.

"What?" she said sharply.

"I spoke to you yesterday," he said. "On the phone? About your brother, Major?"

There was a momentary pause and Ramsgill could now see the little boy, clinging to the woman's leg.

"I told you I was trying to find a friend of mine."

"So?" she said.

"My name's Ramsgill," he said. "Jamie Ramsgill." He pushed a card up to the gate but she didn't take it.

"Have the police contacted you?" he said.

Her eyelids hung low over tired eyes. She then nodded with a single jerk of her head.

"Then you've heard about your brother?"

Her eyes remained impassive, confirming that she had.

"I'm sorry," he said. "I know your brother was mixed up in something, Ms. Devero. With my friend, David. Major painted a copy of a famous painting twenty years ago, and my friend used it to get the real painting, which is worth several million dollars. I don't believe that Major knew what my friend intended to do with the copy; in fact I'm sure he thought he was doing nothing illegal. But what matters now is that your brother was murdered, and—"

"And why do you care?"

"Well, I . . . " Why did he care, Ramsgill thought to himself? Bernice Devero had lost a brother, killed in cold blood. Ramsgill had lost nothing, except a night's worth of sleep and a belief that the world was a pretty good place. He had more than this woman would ever have, and yet here he was, trying to use her to help him out of a jam.

"I . . . I was there last night," he stammered. "I went to try to save your brother's life. But I never should have been there in the first place, especially since I did no good. When I called you yesterday I was looking for my friend, to try to help him out of a bad state. But then I realized that he wasn't the person I'd always thought he was, and that your brother was in trouble. I'm here because I'm trying to find out what happened. What really happened."

Bernice Devero's chest heaved, and she took in a lungful of air. She stood behind the iron gate like an immovable rock.

"When did you talk to your brother last?" Ramsgill asked.

She didn't answer.

"Did you know that he knew David Laycutt? Or that he sent Laycutt a letter asking for money? I have a copy of the letter and Laycutt did make a big withdrawal from his bank account. Ms. Devero, if you know something and you could help me . . . it's just that—"

Ramsgill stopped midsentence, realizing he was talking to air. But even more so, he realized that he had no right to come into this woman's life, no more than he had Claudia Farber's.

"I'm sorry," he said. "Look, I shouldn't even be here."

He stepped down to the sidewalk and back over to his car. He pulled open the door and was about to get in when he looked over to her. She stared at him, then surprised him with a question.

"You know a man named Chatfield?" she said.

"What?"

"Chatfield," she repeated.

"Yeah," said Ramsgill. "At least I know who he is. He used to work at a museum in the city. Why?"

"He called me today," she said.

"And?"

"He said he know who killed Major."

"Yeah?"

Her eyes had begun to well up but they refused to yield tears. The boy looked up at her sadly, but Ramsgill realized there was no way he understood why she was upset.

"Your friend," she said. "He said your friend killed him."

Ramsgill nodded, feeling inadequate to respond in any other way. "David? Did he say how he knew?"

"No. Just said he was awfully sorry. Said he'd been a teacher of Major's at the Pennsylvania Academy. You know Major went to art school."

"I do," said Ramsgill. "And I know that he was a very talented painter."

She sighed, then cast a glance down the block to the activity on the corner.

"He got out of here, didn't he?" she said.

Ramsgill could see the pain on her face, and he wondered what her life must be like. He couldn't imagine raising a child in this place, knowing that whatever you do, by the time the kid is thirteen, he basically has two choices. Withstand the pressures of the street, in which case the reward might be a minimum-wage job for the rest of your life, or succumb to the street and make a ton of money dealing drugs, winding up dead by the time you're twenty-five.

"What's your boy's name?" he said.

"This is Daryl," she said softly.

Daryl nudged his head into the folds of her jeans.

"He don't talk much," she said. "Especially today."

"Who can blame him?" said Ramsgill.

"You say you were at Major's last night?" she said.

Ramsgill nodded.

"Me and Daryl going to have to get up there to get Major's belongings, I expect. The bank'll take back his house. He had a second mortgage on it, you know. And that'll be it."

"I suppose," said Ramsgill.

"Major was a good man," she said, near tears. "He always helped Daryl and me. Just yesterday he spoke to me about getting us out of here."

"Really?"

"Yes," she said, removing her glasses and wiping her eyes. "He told me he was coming into some money. Said he was supposed to get it last night. I told the police about that."

"That would have been the blackmail money."

"No, it wouldn't," she snapped. "That's what you don't understand. Major wouldn't blackmail nobody. He as good as they come.

Major made it out of here and went to college. He always avoided doing wrong."

"Did Major make a decent living from his painting?" said Ramsgill.

"No," she said. "But he loved it. And he didn't need much money. He didn't have no family except us and he lived a simple life."

"Well maybe he didn't consider it blackmail," Ramsgill said. "Like I said, I don't think he knew of Laycutt and Farber's plot when he originally painted his copy. He probably thought that he was doing nothing wrong. And as far as the seventy-five thousand dollars goes, he probably figured that he was just getting a small reward, because the two of them were making a fortune."

She shook her head again. "Not Major," she said.

Ramsgill considered her statement. He could understand why she felt as she did, given that she had just found out he was dead. She was undoubtedly in denial.

"Did he ever talk to you about Laycutt or Farber?"

"Farber was the doctor, right?" Ramsgill nodded.

"No," she said. "He never talked about him. But I know who he is. He the one who gave Major that prize."

"And when you spoke to Major yesterday, he didn't say anything about them?"

"Uh-uh. But ask the museum man. He said he knew about your friend."

"I will," said Ramsgill. "By the way, did you tell the police that Chatfield called?"

"Not yet," she said.

"All right, Ms. Devero. Thank you very much. You take care of yourself. And Daryl too."

The boy's eyes perked up for a moment, perhaps happy that Ramsgill was leaving. He then turned and disappeared into the house, followed by his mother. Ramsgill couldn't help but think of their home as the eye of a very nasty hurricane. He hopped back into his car and started the engine, still consumed by feelings of guilt.

Eleven

*E*lena?" Jamie Ramsgill removed his dialing finger from the cellular handset and tucked the phone beneath his ear. He pulled out around a line of traffic, red taillights syncopating as the line stalled.

"Jamie, where are you?"

"I'm on the expressway, heading out to Chester County," he said. "Why?"

"According to Anne Holden that's where Hayes Chatfield lives now. In a retirement home."

"Who's Hayes Chatfield?"

"He's the man who originally looked at Mrs. Addison's Eakins painting. The one who labeled it a fake. Major Devero's sister told me that he also knows Laycutt killed Devero, but more importantly *why*. I want to talk to him before I turn myself in."

"So you *are* going to turn yourself in? You know Michael called the police this morning."

"Yeah, Cate told me. Big brother watching out for me."

"He's worried about you, Jamie. I am too."

"I'm fine," he said. "Stop worrying. But look, I need you to do something for me. Actually, two things."

"What?"

"First, don't tell Cate or Michael where I'm headed. I'll call Michael when I'm done with Chatfield."

"Okay. What else?"

"Where's Marilyn?"

"She's with a customer."

"Could you get away from the gallery for a little while?"

"I haven't gone to lunch yet."

"It might take longer than that."

"What do you want me to do?"

"I want you to go to City Hall. There's an office somewhere in there that's called the County Recorder of Deeds. I want you to look up a deed."

"How do I do that?"

"They have people who will help you," he said. "What you're looking for is the deed for Seven twenty-one North Pascal Street in the city. I've already traced it back to April of 1963. That's when a man named Tom Mulrooney bought it. When you find that deed, trace it backwards in time through the recording books. I'm interested in knowing who owned the building around 1908, and who owned it in between."

"Why?"

"Because Mrs. Addison's painting was found in that building, and it's also probable that that's where the actual painting was made. Somehow I think Mrs. Addison knew that. And there's still all of this weird business about her keeping the painting a secret, and then not nailing Laycutt when she realized he had duped her."

"Okay. You want me to call you when I get it?"

"*If* you get it," said Ramsgill. "It's apparently not the fastest process in the world. But if I don't hear from you in an hour or so, I'll phone you again."

"Marilyn won't like that."

"The hell with Marilyn. This is important, Elena. I'm very close here."

"Be careful."

"I will. I love you."

"Love you too."

Longmeadow Nursing Home was on the fringes of exurbia, in a part of Chester County that had managed to remain rural for three centuries, but which was now succumbing. What once had been rolling farmland and hunt country was giving way to an ever-expanding universe of urbanization, of which Philadelphia was the core. Revolutionary-era farmhouses were set hard against country roads, but most of them were now fronted by high fences or berms planted in evergreens, to screen out the bellow of traffic. Telephone poles were cluttered with signs for ubiquitous new housing subdivisions. Convenience stores and gas stations were springing up at intersections like dandelions, foreshadowing the inevitable shopping centers and office parks that would follow. Soon the roads would be widened to four lanes, shopping centers would be superseded by malls, and people who had moved here to get a taste of country life would scratch their heads, wondering just why they had moved in the first place.

Longmeadow itself was tasteful, built on the grounds of an old farm. An enormous stone bank barn met visitors as they crossed a stone bridge entering the property, and the main building, though it was contemporary, had the appearance of an agricultural structure. Ramsgill parked in the visitors' lot, which was less than a quarter full. He took the long concrete ramp up to the front entrance, and at the reception desk he was directed by a pleasant woman to a dayroom down a succession of halls that were bathed in the odor of antiseptic. He sat down on a wicker sofa in a pool of sunlight, near windows that overlooked a back lawn.

A few minutes later a nurse rolled an elderly man to the door. The man dismissed her with a flourish, seemingly embarrassed at having to be tended to.

"It's about time you people showed up," he said. "I called you nearly two hours ago."

"Called us?" Ramsgill said.

"Yeah. You are the police, aren't you?"

"No," Ramsgill said, shaking his head. "My name's Jamie Ramsgill. I think you know my sister-in-law, Cate Chew."

Ramsgill stood and offered his hand. The old man took it, cradling it between long bony fingers. He looked up at Ramsgill with watery eyes.

Hayes Chatfield had the face of an aged Shakespearean actor. It was long and tapered, with dark gray eyes. His nose was long too, separated from his mouth by two deep grooves that flared outward from the nose like the mainstays of a sailboat. He had a curious upturned mouth that was set close to his chin. Short gray bangs lay across a lined forehead, and the tops of his ears stood out like the handles of a teacup. He wore a black turtleneck and gold corduroy trousers, the trousers hanging on legs that were as thin as broom handles.

"I know Cate," he said feebly. "She was just beginning at the museum about the time I retired from the academy. If I recall, she borrowed one of our George Bellows for an exhibit she did on sports paintings."

Ramsgill nodded. He vaguely recalled the exhibit.

"But what are you doing here?" Chatfield said.

"I'm interested in what you told Bernice Devero," said Ramsgill. "About her brother's death."

Ramsgill sat again, noticing that Chatfield's skin was almost transparent, practically purple at the extremities of his nose and mouth. He explained how he was mixed up in Laycutt's disappearance and what he had learned in the last twenty-four hours.

"What did you mean when you told Bernice Devero that it was Laycutt who had killed Major?"

"Just that," Chatfield said. "Major told me a long time ago that this might happen. I guess it was twenty years ago. . . . I was brought a painting to look at by Elinor Addison."

"The lost version of Eakins' *William Rush Carving.*"

"Correct. Or so I thought at the time. Anyway, Addison wanted me to look at it, to see if I could authenticate it for her."

"And?"

Chatfield's sagging eyes wandered out the window, squinting at the sunlight.

"And I did . . . look at it . . . that is. I'd have to say, too, that for a while I wasn't sure if it was real or not."

"But you concluded it was fake."

"Yes. It was a good one, but nevertheless a fake. And I've seen many in my day. Years ago . . . long before Mrs. Addison, Bob Pepper of Franklin Mutual came to me with three pieces of Roman sculpture he had bought on approval. He asked me whether they were real or not. One was a marble sarcophagus, supposedly Etruscan. One was a gladiator from the Hellenistic period. The other a bust of the poet Hesiod, from a different period. So I started looking at them, and ancient art isn't even my area. . . ."

He paused, a grimace implanting itself on his long face.

"Am I boring you?" he said.

"No, no," Ramsgill said.

"Okay," Chatfield continued with a huff. "I soon discovered that all three pieces had a curious marking on them—a small indentation in the form of a scythe. As it turned out, with the help of the Philadelphia police, we uncovered an entire ring of forgers. They had a sculptor who had apprenticed in Italy. He knew the techniques of ancient sculpture, and how to age stone and so forth. He would go to great lengths. Sometimes he used old stone, sometimes he would take a completed piece and smash it up to create fragments. He would dip the marble into acid baths up to forty times to pockmark them. He would cover them with dirt, then polish them to fabricate a patina. An art dealer on Washington Square sold them as originals. The sculptor's problem was that he was also an artist. He couldn't resist putting a bit of himself into the work. Do you know what his name was?"

Ramsgill shook his head.

"Falce, Nicoletto Falce. *Falce* means scythe in Italian. I told Pepper to return the statues to the dealer posthaste. Eventually, both Falce and the dealer pled guilty to fraud."

"That's interesting," said Ramsgill. "How about the Eakins painting? Did it have the forger's signature?"

"Not a blatant one. But it was there."

Chatfield paused, and looked again out the window. He smiled at a blaze of forsythia at the edge on the grassy knoll behind the nursing home.

"What was I talking about?"

"Signatures," said Ramsgill.

"Oh yes. You must know that Eakins was meticulous about detail. The forger fudged the detail of a chair in the painting. He'd put a Boston chair in, which Major later admitted to me was his signature."

"But how did you know it was Major?"

"I didn't really, until I confronted him. You see, Major had been a student of mine at the academy. When I was examining the painting I realized that the canvas, even though it was quite old, was stretched with double folds at the stretcher boards. That technique was unknown in the nineteenth century, in fact a technique I have only seen a couple of painters use in my entire life. One of them was Major."

"So what'd you do?"

"I called him, and asked him to come see me. I had the painting in my office, and the minute he walked in, he nearly fainted. I knew right then and there that he had painted it. It didn't take long before he admitted what he had done."

"So what'd you do then?"

Chatfield was staring at Ramsgill.

"He was ashamed. He told me about Laycutt and Farber, but said that he'd had no idea what they had intended to do with his work. He asked if I'd hold off in telling Mrs. Addison, until he could talk to them. A couple of days later he came back and told me he had confronted Laycutt. But Laycutt had threatened him. I thought Major meant Laycutt'd threatened to bring Major down with him, which he had, but Laycutt also physically threatened him."

"And what was your reaction?"

"I did something you'll probably think was contemptible. I told Addison it was a forgery, but I never let on who was responsible for it. Don't ask me why. I guess I didn't like her to begin with. I'd been the brunt of her drunken tirades at museum functions once too often, and besides, she hadn't paid that much for the painting anyway. She told me that when she brought it to me. And I liked Major. I believed his story that he had no idea that the copy he had made was going to be used to defraud her. I couldn't expose him. Hell, he'd been through the mill at that point."

"And what about today?" Ramsgill said. "Why are you so sure that it was Laycutt who killed him?"

"Who the hell else would it be? And then to find out that Farber is dead too. That's too much of a coincidence."

Chatfield's hands rested on the wheelchair armrests. The index finger of his right hand tapped slowly. Ramsgill nodded, then slowly rose.

"Mr. Chatfield, you've been very helpful."

Chatfield grabbed his hand between both of his own, pulling him slightly closer.

"Tell your sister hello."

Sister-*in-law*, Ramsgill thought, but he didn't say anything. Instead, he left Chatfield at the edge of the day room, humming some unrecognizable tune, his eyes looking out the windows to a romantic landscape of the way Pennsylvania used to be.

Ramsgill pulled out of the nursing home parking lot feeling a sense of relief. Chatfield had driven the final nail into Laycutt's coffin, confirming what Ramsgill thought he already knew. As he took back roads to Route 202, he thought about getting some sleep, wondering how long he would have to stay at police headquarters once he turned himself in. He phoned Michael at the law firm but was told that he was in a deposition. Since he had a forty-five-minute drive back to town anyway, Ramsgill told Michael's secretary that it wasn't urgent, but that when he got a chance, Michael should call him back on the car phone. He then hung up and phoned Elena at the gallery. She wasn't back from City Hall, and from the tone of Marilyn Foster's voice, Foster wasn't too pleased. He decided not to leave a message.

For the rest of the drive he tried to fit together the whole puzzle, the few remaining pieces of which had fallen more or less into place. There was still the curious notion of Farber's having given the painting to the museum, but by now, Ramsgill had all but decided that it was a ploy to exonerate himself. And there was the discrepancy of the money, but he was sure that sooner or later the police would sort that out. Just as they would sort out the appearance that Ramsgill might have had something to do with Devero's death. Everything else fit into place.

When he turned north onto 202, he suddenly became mired in traffic. It was only a little after two, but work was being done on the highway, and up ahead in the distance he could see that the traffic was being funneled into a single lane. He played yo-yo for a while with the other cars, and little by little, made it to King of Prussia.

He was just getting on the Schuylkill when the phone beeped.

"Michael?"

He listened through static to the sound of coins being inserted into a pay phone, and then he spoke again. "Hello? Michael?"

"This isn't Michael."

The voice on the other end of the line sent chilled vibrations up his back, as if a razor blade were running along his spine. It was the low voice of David Laycutt, devoid of emotion or any semblance of warmth. All at once Ramsgill's hands were clammy.

"Jamie? I know you're there."

"I am." Ramsgill swallowed hard, feeling trapped by the phone connection. He didn't want to speak to Laycutt; he wanted nothing to do with him.

"I want to meet, Jamie," the voice said. In Ramsgill's mind it was just that, a voice, not the person Ramsgill had known for twenty-five years.

"I don't think so," said Ramsgill.

"I have to talk to you, Jamie."

"I *really* don't think so," repeated Ramsgill.

"I didn't kill them. I saw your note when I got back to my mountain house last night, and I know if you went there then you must think the worst. But you've got to believe me."

Ramsgill listened, accelerating up an access ramp.

"Meet me in Fairmount Park," Laycutt said.

"David, that's ridiculous. There's no way in hell I'm meeting you in Fairmount Park."

"Then you don't believe me?"

"Christ, David. You got a blackmail letter from Devero. You withdrew money from the bank. You must have bought a gun. And . . . and you called Farber. What am I supposed to think?"

"Jamie, listen to me. Listen carefully. I didn't do it. I'll tell you that a thousand times, but you've got to believe me."

"And you didn't arrange to have the Eakins forgery made? You didn't make the swap? You didn't threaten Devero? What the hell was it you had on Mrs. Addison, anyway, to keep her quiet?"

Now, the other end of the line went silent. All Ramsgill could hear was Laycutt's breathing.

"I'll admit to some of that," the voice said. "But couldn't we talk about it? Remember, it was Devero who sent me the letter."

"So that justified killing him?"

"Just meet me on Belmont Plateau. Fifteen minutes is all I need."

"David, I'm going to the police. I've seen more hell in the last twenty-four hours than I hope to ever see in my life. I'm sick of it, of being any part of it. I was reluctant to act because I thought you were in trouble. So did Tod. And because we were sympathetic, two people are dead. That's something I'll have to live with for the rest of my life."

The phone clicked twice, then Laycutt came back on in a sea of static.

"Jamie? I'm going to be on Belmont Plateau at three-thirty. At Belmont Mansion. All I ask is five minutes. If you've ever had any feeling for me whatsoever, you'll believe me when I'm telling you that this isn't a con. I'll be there. You be there too."

Twelve

*M*ichael Ramsgill," the voice on the other end of the line said.

"It's Jamie, Michael."

"Where are you?"

"I'm heading into town."

He was traveling on a stretch of the expressway just outside the city limits. The old mill town of Manayunk was strung out across the hills on the other side of the river, like wash hanging on a line.

"We've been looking for you all day," said Michael. He was speaking in the austere voice of a teacher, or a parent upset with a child.

"I know you have. And you broke your promise."

"Jamie, you know this is for your own good."

"Yeah, right."

"What's the matter?"

Ramsgill braked as he came up behind a slow-moving station wagon, unable to move around it because of the volume of traffic in the passing lane.

"I just got a call from Laycutt. I'm a little upset."

"Where was he?"

"Sounded like a pay phone."

"What'd he say?"

"He said he wanted to meet me. I told him he was nuts."

"Where'd he want to meet?"

"On Belmont Plateau."

"Then he wants a secluded spot."

"Right. So he can use me as a human pin cushion. I'll have to admit, Michael, I'm scared. The sooner I get to your office, the better."

"So you're coming in?"

"Yes."

"What did Laycutt say, though? Why'd he want to meet?"

"He admitted that he had arranged the forgery and the theft of Mrs. Addison's painting, but he denies that he had anything to do with Farber or Devero's death. Said he just wants to talk."

"And how'd he sound?"

"I'd say desperate, but his voice was so drained of emotion that it was hard to tell."

"Did he arrange a time to meet?"

"Why does it matter? There's no way I'm going up there."

The line went silent for a moment before Jamie spoke again.

"Michael? What are you thinking?"

"Jamie, there's no doubt that coming in is the safe thing to do. But I just got off the phone with Guntherson. He believes everything I've told him about you, and he wants Laycutt. Since Laycutt called you from a pay phone, and since he wants to meet in the park, that means he's still in the city. If you don't show, he might flee for good."

"So what?"

"Do you want to catch this guy?"

"Sure, but . . ."

"What time did he say to meet?"

"Three thirty. He said he'd be at Belmont Mansion. I suppose he thinks the place will be empty, since it's a weekday."

"Listen to this, Jamie, and if you don't agree with it, fine. But I could call Gunterson back right now and get law enforcement up there. I could come up too. It's two forty now, and we could be there when you arrive. It's our one chance to catch him, Jamie. The only downside is that you'd have to play guinea pig."

Jamie took a deep breath, remembering the pain of being blindsided by Laycutt at Devero's house. He was afraid, but he also wanted to hear Laycutt's story. Somewhere in one of his mind's alcoves, he still didn't see Laycutt as a cold-blooded killer. Was there any chance that he had been telling the truth on the phone?

"How about it?"

"I don't know, Michael."

"We've got to move quick, Jamie."

"Fine. Call them. But so help me, Michael, they'd better come through."

"They will," Michael said. "Look, why don't you do this? Show up at three thirty-five. He'll wait that long. Park right in front of the garden. We want to know when you arrive and you want him to see that you're alone."

"Okay."

"Don't worry, Jamie. I'll take care of it."

You'd better, Jamie thought, you damned well better.

David Laycutt looked in the rearview mirror, the narrow rectangle framing his pink eyes. He moved his head slightly from side to side, then up and down, until he had navigated his whole face. What he saw disturbed him. It wasn't an unattractive face, and it wasn't like he didn't see it four or five or six times a day. But it occurred to him just now, abruptly and absurdly, that he was middle-aged. His chin had lost its definition. His hair had receded halfway back across his doughy round head. His eyes were the same as they had been when he was twenty, but now, they peered out through folds of skin and pockets of brown. The mole on his left cheek seemed to be growing larger. Was it his imagination, or should he see a dermatologist to check it for malignancy?

He laughed. Who are you kidding, David? You'll be lucky to see a doctor once every three months in prison. And that's what it all came down to, the prospect of prison.

Would Ramsgill show up? Or would he go to the police like he said he would? And even if he came, would he have what Laycutt needed? He hated lying to Jamie, but he had no choice at this point. Jamie himself hadn't believed a word he had told him, and he was a friend. There wasn't a snowball's chance in hell that he would fare any better with the police.

He sat back in the leather driver's seat, readjusting the mirror to frame the rear window of the car. It was 3:20 P.M. He looked to his left. A panoramic view of the city skyline was fronted by the great sloping lawn of the plateau. The grass was still brown for the most part, but clumps of green had begun to work through, offering signs of spring. The lawn was more or less empty, too early in the season for softball games, too late for cross country skiing or sledding. A few people walked dogs in the distance, but up here, on the drive, there was hardly a soul. That was the way he wanted it. That was his hope.

The car phone beeped again and Ramsgill snatched it up, his stomach as tight as a pair of Spandex shorts.

"Hello," he said. His voice sounded fractured, the ringing of the car phone having broken fifteen minutes of uneasy silence. He was parked out in front of Memorial Hall, a half mile below Belmont Plateau, where he had decided to wait until three-thirty. He had whiled away the time running scenarios over in his mind of what would happen when he came face-to-face with David Laycutt.

"Jamie?" It was Elena.

"Hi." The greeting came out short and sharp, and he regretted it almost immediately.

"What's the matter?" Elena asked.

"Nothing. Nothing's the matter."

"You don't sound good. Where are you?"

"I . . . I'm on the expressway," he said. "Heading to Michael's office." He wasn't about to tell her where he really was, or what he was about to do.

"I have that information for you," she said.

"You do?"

"I went to the City Hall like you asked and tracked that property back to 1900. I have a list of owners. Before Tom Mulrooney it was a man named Scheetz, and before him the Namico Soap Company, and before them—"

"How about who owned it in 1908?"

"I'm getting to that, *mia caro*. I just thought I would string out the suspense."

"I don't have time for stringing out, Elena." He looked at his watch. It was three twenty-two.

"Very well," she said. "In 1908 it was a man named Thomas Eakins. Ever hear of him?"

"You're kidding."

"I'm not. And that explains why the painting was found there. Eakins owned the property from 1894 until 1908."

"He must have used it as a studio," said Ramsgill.

"But that's only one half of the story, Jamie."

"What do you mean?"

"That explains how the painting ended up there in the first place, but it doesn't explain how Mrs. Addison knew it was there, or why, as you said to me earlier, she never blew the whistle on David Laycutt."

"And you've figured that out?"

"*Certamente,*" she replied. "Remember how Cate had said that one of the art historians had suggested a name for the young model in the painting?"

"Right," said Ramsgill. "Bachman or Backman or something."

"How about Beecham?" said Elena. "Grace Beecham."

"Wait a minute. That's the name of Mrs. Addison's mother."

"You are correct, sir."

"She was the model? How the hell . . . ?"

"Patience, Jamie."

Again he looked at his watch.

"Eakins transferred the property to a Grace Beecham in 1908 and she owned it until 1942," Elena said. "Beecham sounded familiar so I called Cate to ask the names that had been suggested for the model, with no idea that Beecham was Mrs. Addison's mother. She told me you had been in this morning. We put two and two together, and there you have it."

"So Mrs. Addison wanted the painting kept a secret because her mother had had an affair?"

"Only partially," said Elena. "There's more to it than that. Cate also told me that you had said that Mrs. Addison's mother was widowed."

"Yes," said Ramsgill. "About the time Mrs. Addison was born."

"Afraid not," said Elena. "The deed that transferred the property to Grace Beecham did not list a husband, nor did it list her as a widow, which I learned from a clerk in the deeds office was customary to have put on a deed back in those days."

"So you're saying that she was single when she got the property?"

"Yes. And remember that in the painting the model looks to be no more than twenty."

"That's right," said Ramsgill. "I saw a picture of Mrs. Beecham that was taken at her daughter's wedding, from 1931. She couldn't have been much more than forty. So I guess she fits."

"Actually, she would have been forty-one in 1931," said Elena.

"How do you know that?"

"Because I saw Elinor Addison's birth certificate. It lists the mother's birthdate. Mrs. Beecham was born in 1890."

Ramsgill noticed that it was three twenty-five. He rolled up his window and started the car.

"You've lost me now," he said.

"After I hung up with Cate," she said, "I told the young fellow at the deeds office about the story. He's the one who had told me that 'widow' would have been listed on the deed. He said that he loved these old stories, and that if you keep digging, you sometimes come up with gold. He told me point-blank that if a man in those days transferred property to a single woman who was unrelated to him, then it was because he had some sort of financial obligation to her."

"You mean, like he was paying to support her?"

"Her. Or her and her children. If she had any."

"Go on."

"You told Cate that Mrs. Addison was from an old Philadelphia family," said Elena. "And that her father had died in a sailing accident."

"That's what Anne Holden told me."

"What else did she tell you?"

"That her uncle's side of the family were social register types, that they were very conscious of blue blood hierarchy."

The line went quiet for a couple of seconds.

"Then that explains it," said Elena.

"What?"

"Why Mrs. Addison never let on about the painting until she suspected it was a fake. And why even then, she never brought charges against Laycutt. Because she would have been exposing herself, you see. She wasn't from a proper family, Jamie, and she must have hid that from everyone around her. Including her husband."

Ramsgill by now had pulled out into the street, turning right onto Belmont Drive.

"And you're saying all this because you believe that it was Mrs. Addison's mother in the painting?"

"I'm saying that, yes. But like I said, I also saw Elinor Addison's birth certificate, Jamie. My friend at the deeds office put me onto that. She was born in Philadelphia in 1908. And her mother was not the only one in the painting who was related to her. Her father, as it turns out, was in the painting too."

Jamie Ramsgill eased up on the gas pedal, just at the point where the drive curved to his left, disappearing into deep shadowed green. To his right, the convex side of the curve opened out to a panorama of the city, the serrated skyline some four miles in the distance, fronted by lawn that cascaded down to ball fields and picnic grounds. To his left, the inside of the curve, the sloped roof of Belmont Mansion peaked above a continuous line of woody privet hedge. Surrounding the property, just outside the privet, was a chain-link fence. A blue plywood sign noted that the house was under renovation, and Ramsgill now figured Laycutt had known that fact when he set up their meeting.

The fence made it impossible for Ramsgill to park in front of the house. Instead he drove until he found the entrance to a small parking lot, just beyond the house on the left. The parking lot was empty except for a light green office trailer and a dark Acura Legend—four door, with a tan leather interior. Ramsgill pulled up beside the car, aware that from this vantage point Michael and the police might not know that he had arrived. A thick canopy of trees hung over the parking lot, and it was screened from the house by additional planting. A break in the green revealed a chain-link gate.

As he approached he could see that the house was a tall block of painted yellow brick, with keystoned windows and corners wrapped in quoins. Teetering shutters flanked windows in need of reglazing. The standing-seam copper roof had oxidized to light turquoise green and was ripped in more than one location. A piece of the front porch roof was collapsed.

A breeze weaved its way through the trees, creating a soft rhythmical sound. The afternoon sun washed the house, and Ramsgill entered a side yard, now completely surrounded by hedge and building. He turned left and walked cautiously toward the front of the house, the side that faced the city. He rounded the corner of the dilapidated porch, and found a small front yard, the privet creating a wall between the house and the drive beyond. He was in a secluded world.

Suddenly he heard a low trill and the clap of wings as a pigeon lit from a window on the second floor. His eyes jerked up to the window, which was half dressed, a louvered shutter flanking only its left side. He squinted against the low sun, wondering if it were the police or Michael who had startled the bird from behind the window. But all he saw were the wavy ripples of handblown glass, the room beyond obscure.

He then took a deep breath and continued around the house. He climbed a step up to the wooden porch and looked down its length. At the end, an open doorway led into the house.

He stepped inside, turning, coming immediately upon a cavernous room. The walls were stripped bare of plaster, horizontal wooden lath showing like ribs through a lean torso. It was cold inside, and dead quiet. Light trickled in from a pair of far windows. On one wall was a fireplace, and next to it a stack of lumber and a few plastic containers of patching compound. A metal trough encrusted with dried cement leaned against the skeletal wall.

"Jamie."

The voice seemed to come from nowhere, just appeared like a flash of gunpowder. Ramsgill's head snapped in the direction of a far stair, and all at once he saw the tall broad body of David Laycutt. A tide of adrenaline rose through Ramsgill like a glass being filled with electric Kool-Aid.

David Laycutt was standing in a doorway at the base of the stair. He wore a spread-collared shirt that looked as if it had been slept in and rumpled trousers with mud the color of creamed coffee on the cuffs. His eyes looked like he had been on a three-day drinking binge. His long arms hung languidly at his sides, and the fingers of his right hand twitched against his tapered thigh.

"I thought you'd come," he said. His voice was some odd amalgam of fear and giddiness, like that of a kid asking a girl for the first dance at a junior high social. It was made all the more strange by the surreal echo of the empty house.

"Tell me," said Ramsgill. "How'd you know Mrs. Addison was Eakins' illegitimate daughter?"

Laycutt's jaw widened, an almost invisible grin forming on his lips. He took two steps into the room. Ramsgill stiffened, and Laycutt stopped, realizing that Jamie wanted him to come no closer than he already was.

"I found a letter at her house," Laycutt said. "When I was working for her. It was from her mother. It had been written in the early fifties, not long before Grace Beecham died. It explained it all. How her father hadn't died in an accident, how she and Eakins had been lovers, how Eakins had supported them after Elinor was born. Ms. Beecham had fallen in love with him when she was still a teenager, when she had secretly acted as his model."

"And so you decided that it was all right to bilk her daughter."

"Oh, come on, Jamie. The woman was a basket case. Her reality came from the bottom of a vodka bottle."

Ramsgill tried to connect Laycutt's voice with his words. It was like hearing one of those propaganda tapes in which the enemy forces a downed pilot to say things you know he doesn't mean. Could Laycutt really be so cruel?

"So you approached Farber," Ramsgill continued. "How much did Devero's forgery cost you?"

"Facsimile, Jamie. It cost twenty thousand dollars."

"Paid for by Farber."

"Correct."

"And what was the deal between you two? Did you get money up front or were you to split the profits?"

"Both. I needed money back then, Jamie. The firm was struggling, but there was no way in hell that I was going to give up on it and go back to work for someone else."

"But you say you were going to get more money when Farber sold the painting. Is that when you made up your mind to kill him, after he decided to bequeath the painting to the museum?"

"I told you I didn't kill him."

"Then why don't you give yourself up?"

"You don't believe me, Jamie, and you're a friend. How the hell do you think the police are going to react?"

For the first time Ramsgill noticed a rise in pitch in Laycutt's voice.

"How about Devero then?"

"I didn't kill him either, Jamie."

"But you'd threatened to kill him. Hayes Chatfield told me that."

Laycutt's eyes caved in, before a long exasperating sigh.

"And I might have," he said. "I did go to his house. But there's a lot of distance between threatening someone and killing them. By the time I got there he was already dead."

"How do you know?"

"The place was crawling with police. I drove right by."

A bubble of laughter rose up from Ramsgill's throat.

"And they weren't there because you called them?" he said. "To frame me?"

"Jamie, I had no idea that it was you. . . . I mean . . . no I didn't call them."

Ramsgill weighed the answer, considering his accumulation of truths, half-truths, and lies, trying to figure out where this one fit.

"Let me ask you again. How did you know Devero was dead?"

"I just did. . . . I . . . well, I knew that something bad had happened. And then I went back to my cabin and realized that you'd been there. I learned about Major this morning. On the radio, as I was driving back to the city."

Laycutt's fingers again launched into a tap dance on his thigh. Ramsgill's eyes traveled the empty room, his ears trying to pick up any sign of Michael and the police.

"David," he said. "You're the only person who had a conceivable motive to kill them. Devero was killed at the precise time you were to meet him. He'd sent you, and you only, the note. And you'd tried to track Farber down earlier in the day."

"*Goddammit, Jamie!* I'm telling you the truth."

"Then, like I said, turn yourself in."

Laycutt stepped forward again, this time oblivious to any desire Ramsgill might have had for him to keep his distance. He took three steps and rose in Ramsgill's perspective like a thunderhead encapsulating the horizon.

"I'm getting out of here, Jamie. I've got to go somewhere far away."

Ramsgill stepped backward until he was close to a wall.

"And you have something that belongs to me," Laycutt continued. "You can either give it to me, or I can take it away."

"I don't know what you're talking about," said Ramsgill.

Laycutt's brow pinched down.

"I want the letter," Laycutt barked.

Ramsgill swallowed, feeling very small in Laycutt's towering presence. Where the hell was Michael? He'd promised they'd be here.

"I don't have it, David."

"Don't bullshit me," Laycutt said. His eyes were now staring down at Ramsgill like cauldrons of pig iron.

"I don't. I swear. . . . "

Laycutt slipped a pistol from his pocket, a little thing that was

cobalt blue with a short snub barrel. He held it waist high, which, because of Laycutt's height, meant that it was pointed at Ramsgill's
chest.

"Give me the letter, Jamie."

"I don't have it."

"This isn't a joke."

"I don't, I said. I gave it to my—"

"Brother," shot a familiar voice, cutting through the tense air.

Both Laycutt and Jamie turned to see Michael Ramsgill step out of
the shadows of another side room, holding his own gun at his waist.
He looked mildly absurd, Jamie thought, dressed in an English-cut
suit, with his nine-thousand-dollar watch inches away from a semiautomatic.

"Put the gun down," Michael said.

"Who are you?"

"Jamie's brother."

Laycutt looked back to Jamie, as if he had been betrayed.

"You didn't think I'd meet you alone," said Jamie. "Where are the
police, Michael?"

Michael didn't answer, only cocking his head slightly, an indication
that they weren't here.

"The gun, Mr. Laycutt."

All of a sudden David Laycutt thrust out his left arm, closing the
distance between him and his old friend in a fraction of a second. He
corralled Jamie by the shoulder, spinning him like a dance partner
until he was between himself and Ramsgill's brother. Ramsgill's heart
was thumping now, and he was mad, mad at Laycutt for being such a
fool, mad at his brother for not getting the police here. His life was in
the hands of a fifty-one-year-old attorney who held a pistol as uncomfortably as a Muslim might hold a beer.

"Let him go," said Michael. It wasn't a command, more of a plea,
and not a very lawyerly one. Jamie noticed his brother swallow, and
the gun begin to waver. Laycutt reached his hand forward, pointing
his pistol at Michael. Jamie, seeing a single momentary opportunity
to do something, brought his hand down on Laycutt's wrist. Laycutt's
strength overwhelmed him though and immediately he was flailing
backwards. He stumbled to the floor, rolled once, then was up again.
Laycutt sent a shot in Michael's direction, and Michael disappeared
into an open doorway. Two more shots rang out, then Laycutt turned

toward Jamie. Time slowed as the gun pivoted in his direction; Ramsgill could see the black hole at the end of the barrel with perfect clarity, and then the hideous scowl on Laycutt's face as he jabbed the gun towards Jamie. A veil of gray puffed from the barrel as if it were a cigar, and then came the sound, an explosive pop that was almost simultaneous with the searing pain.

Jamie flinched as he was punched backwards, reeling like a water boy who has inadvertently stepped out onto the gridiron and met a linebacker head on. His shirt ripped open and blood, as red and shiny as Chinese lacquer, spread across the white cloth. He spun sideways and down again, and the room seemed to close in on him, but he knew that if he didn't get up again he would be dead. He remembered being in Devero's house the night before, and how he had found Laycutt's leg in the dark. He now charged forward again, this time with the benefit of light, right toward him, right toward the gun.

When their bodies collided Ramsgill's speed and momentum overcame Laycutt's size. Laycutt gave way like a balloon losing air and Ramsgill drove him backward into the pile of lumber, which crackled as it collapsed. The buckets of compound and the metal trough collapsed too, and Ramsgill found himself on top of Laycutt, pounding his fists into Laycutt's midsection, with Laycutt unable to keep him at bay. Three times he swept a fist across Laycutt's huge jaw, and each time Laycutt was unable to stop him. Blood flew from the extremities of Laycutt's mouth. But then Laycutt seemed to find a reserve. He wriggled out from under Ramsgill and all at once was above him.

"*You fuck!*" he screamed, his face now convulsing in rage, his body electrified. He brought the gun down on Ramsgill's forehead, thrusting it against his skull. Ramsgill's side shrieked with pain, but he knew that it meant nothing. His side would be forgotten soon. It was over, the curtain was about to fall.

The last thing he saw before the shot was Laycutt mouthing two words.

You're dead, he said.

And then the sound of gunfire again, a sharp, hideous pop, repeated again and again as echo. But this time it was Laycutt's face that seized up in horror. A second passed in slow time, and then Laycutt's chest lurched forward like a locomotive, his mouth fell open, and he looked down at Ramsgill, the pistol dropping from his hand. Once again his eyes accused Ramsgill of betrayal, and then they seemed to implore

Ramsgill's aid. His head became unsteady and began to wobble, followed by the slump of his shoulders, just before he rolled off Ramsgill and fell backward to the floor.

Ramsgill struggled to lift his head. Behind Laycutt's body was Michael, shaking like a leaf in a windstorm and with the gun still pointed in Laycutt's direction. Ramsgill wanted to reach out and hug him, but he realized just how big of a hypocrite that would make him. They stood staring at one another across the cold, dark space, connected by a bond they hadn't shared in years. Blood was thicker than water, Ramsgill realized, the gushing hole in his side notwithstanding.

Thirteen

T ime, in the axiomatic sense, heals old wounds.

Three months passed before the matter of the Eakins painting returned to the forefront of Ramsgill's consciousness. By then the bruises on his face had long since disappeared, and the gunshot wound to his abdomen was slowly healing. Time had also given Ramsgill and Michael a chance to reflect on their relationship, which for so long, like a garden overrun with weeds, had gone untended. Ramsgill himself had offered the first olive branch at the hospital two days after the incident on Belmont Plateau. No doubt his opinion of Michael had been softened somewhat by the fact that his brother had saved his life.

Michael accepted Jamie's entreaty, and they talked through some things that had long been buried in their relationship. He apologized to Jamie for not contacting him when their father was dying. He also apologized for having left Jamie to be with his father, back when he was a teenager. He changed in other ways too, but then looking down the barrel of a gun does that to people. Though three months is hardly a lifetime, Michael seemed to lose some of his preoccupation with work, and perhaps with things monetary. He and Cate took two weeks off for a trip to Block Island, returning invigorated. Jamie was offered a position by Tod Farr at Laycutt's old firm and accepted it. He and Elena bought a building in the city, and by mid July, they were back in town for good.

On a sultry Saturday evening the week they returned, the Philadel-phia Museum of Art hosted a private cocktail party for the board of trustees and members of the press. Jamie and Elena arrived at the great porch of the museum at dusk, where an army of red-jacketed valets scampered to park a parade of Mercedes and Jaguars. In the museum's main hall a bar and buffet had been set up, and elaborate flower arrangements brought splashes of color to a space otherwise weighed down by giant pillars of beige stone. Champagne glasses clinked like Glockenspiels, filling the grand space with unintended music. The low buzz of party talk rode the stilted museum air. A chamber ensemble played capriccios on the second-floor balcony.

As they walked toward the bar, Elena nudged Ramsgill. In the far corner of the hall, near a Diego Rivera mural, a crowd of thin so-cialites surrounded a younger woman like groupies paying homage to a rock star. Flashes of diamonds were set off by flamboyant designer cocktail dresses, and even from a distance, one sensed the adulation being heaped on the younger woman. It was Cate, now curator of American Art, the person who had brought *William Rush Carving His Allegory of the Schuylkill River* to the museum.

Ramsgill and Elena retrieved a drink and made their way past a cou-ple of television news cameramen, then through a large portal on the left side of the hall. A quieter crowd had gathered in a room that was part of the temporary exhibition space. The room was white, and its walls unadorned. Overhead, a grid of black was broken in just two places by track spots that brought precise beams of light down into the room. The beams were focused on a single object on the far wall, the Eakins painting illuminated in soft splendor like a Madonna and child at the altar of some Renaissance church.

As they approached the painting, a familiar hand fell on Ramsgill's shoulder.

"Hey there."

Ramsgill turned to see Michael, his broad face in an exuberant smile. He was dressed smartly in a shawl-collared dinner jacket, a red damask vest, and black silk tie. He kissed Elena on the cheek.

"You look beautiful, as usual," he said.

"*Grazie tante,*" she replied.

"I want to introduce you to someone," Michael said.

An older gentleman in tortoiseshell eyeglasses with a colorful tie and cummerbund set that looked like a Matisse painting stood beside Michael.

"This is Turner Baltzell," said Michael. "Director of the museum. Turner, my brother, Jamie. And Elena Piruzzi."

Baltzell shook hands vigorously with them both.

"Glad you could be here," he said.

"Congratulations," said Ramsgill. "You must be quite happy."

"Oh yes. This is a coup. We've got the major television stations here tonight. And the papers. We'll play this for all it's worth, then next spring have a true unveiling of the painting for the public. In a blockbuster show. There are people who don't know Eakins from the Easter Bunny, but who will undoubtedly come to see the mystery painting, the one that languished in a warehouse for ninety years before it was discovered. The story has everything. Adultery, fraud, deceit, murder. If that doesn't get them into the doors of this place, nothing will. And once we get them in here, we'll keep them. Membership is already up fifteen percent from last year."

"That's nice," said Ramsgill. In truth, he found it anything but nice. He remembered a time when people went to museums to enjoy art, not to participate in spectacle. When museum directors were expected by their boards to be connoisseurs, not P. T. Barnums. On the other hand, Baltzell was right. If he could get people through the door, it would ultimately help the museum's primary mission—to preserve icons for posterity.

"Of course, none of this would be possible," Baltzell continued, "were it not for your indefatigable sister-in-law. And I suppose it helps that her better half here is a lawyer. It was certainly good timing with Harold Farber."

Ramsgill wasn't listening. His eyes had drifted out of the gallery, back toward the main hall. From where he was standing, he could see the linened buffet table. Hoards of husbands in black tie were raking in hors d'oeuvres, and in the middle of the group was a stunning woman wearing a gold lamé dress that revealed more décolletage than a Victoria's Secret negligee. It took Ramsgill a moment to realize that it was Claudia Farber.

"I have a brilliant idea," said Baltzell. "Michael, maybe your brother here could give us a lecture when the Eakins show opens." Ramsgill looked back to the director. "We have a Wednesday singles night at the museum now. You know, cash bar, music, films, lectures. You could give the group a talk about how you tracked down the Eakins forgers. How you pinned the murders on David Laycutt."

"I didn't pin the murders on anyone," said Ramsgill, his eyes shifting between Claudia Farber and Baltzell. "The police did that. In fact, I still had my doubts. They dropped the case because Laycutt was dead and because circumstantial evidence pointed toward him."

"Whatever," said Baltzell, his own gaze now directed toward the hall. "Oh look. Claudia Farber has come. I didn't know she was still in town."

"Town?" said Michael. "I thought she'd already left the country."

Baltzell shrugged. "I suppose not," he said. "I'd better say hello. It was nice to meet you, Mr. Ramsgill, Ms. Piruzzi, and think about that lecture for me, will you?"

Ramsgill smiled and nodded.

"Michael," asked Ramsgill, as he watched Baltzell stride away, "what did you mean about Claudia Farber's leaving the country?"

"Just that. Cate says she's moving back to Venezuela. Can't say it surprises me. I suppose she'll liquidate Harold's estate and then be gone. Everyone I know thinks that was her intention from the day she met him."

Ramsgill looked back toward the buffet table. He recalled the expression on Claudia Farber's face when Vibeke Lidz had told her about the codicil to her husband's will. Shock would have been putting it too mildly. The look confirmed the possibility of what Michael was now telling him, that she had had designs on Farber's money all along. But if she were upset about losing the painting, she sure didn't seem to be showing it.

"Are you surprised she's here?" he said.

Michael nodded, his lower lip jutting forward. She was now talking to Baltzell, her smile brighter than anything else in the hall.

"Let's take a look at the painting," said Elena. "Before your eyes pop out."

She slapped Ramsgill playfully on the rear and he and his brother snickered before turning together toward the canvas.

And there it was, in all its dark beauty. For the first time it occurred to Ramsgill that a painting had a life not unlike that of a person, one that could be notorious or unremarkable, which in a way, justified

Baltzell's desire to link the Eakins provenance to its exhibition. In the case of the Eakins painting, it began with a secret between a young woman and a master painter, and it ended with one transgression piled upon another until three men were dead. And it was as if the painting could control its own destiny, slipping out of the grasp of Phil Matzkin, Elinor Addison, Anne Holden, Harold Farber, and even that of his young wife, Claudia. But eventually, he supposed, it had ended up where it belonged in the first place, in a museum, to be enjoyed and scrutinized by generations.

"By the way," said Michael, "how'd it go with the sandblasting?"

"What?"

"You know, getting your concrete sandblasted."

"Oh, fine," said Ramsgill. "They say they'll be done by Monday. I hope so, because the mover will only hold our stuff for the weekend. Of course, we'll still be under construction, but at least that'll be out of the way."

"What the hell possessed you two to buy that place anyway?" said Michael. "Who would convert a grain elevator into a place to live?"

Elena laughed. "Only an architect," she said.

"It's not a grain *elevator*," said Jamie. "It's a grain warehouse."

Michael clutched his brother's arm. "Rats come with it?" he said.

"Good evening."

Michael's chiding was interrupted by a soft voice that had crept up behind them. The trio turned to see Claudia Farber standing five feet away. Her lamé dress shimmered like a ballroom crystal and she wore diamond stud earrings the size of dimes.

"Claudia," said Michael.

Farber and Michael exchanged kisses on the cheek.

"And how are you, Mr. Ramsgill. Jamie, isn't it?"

Ramsgill nodded, trying to keep his eyes from straying to her chest.

"Fine," he said.

Elena jabbed Ramsgill in the back.

"Oh, I'm sorry. This is Elena Piruzzi."

They shook hands. Farber was looking beyond Elena, however, at the painting on the wall. She wore the bittersweet look of someone who had just relinquished a love.

"What extraordinary beauty," she said.

They each turned and Ramsgill's eyes were captured by the nude image of Grace Beecham standing atop the block of wood. For the first time it dawned on him that Claudia Farber must have found some affinity for Beecham, as they were both radiant and both had been attached to well-known older men.

"I suppose it does belong here," Farber admitted. "But I'll miss it when I return to Caracas."

"Then you are moving?" said Michael.

"Yes."

"When?"

She shrugged, the slope of her soft, tanned shoulders rising and falling with simple ease.

"One month," she said, "maybe two. I've sold Pennwood, or at least I have an agreement for sale. And we're auctioning off some of Harold's artwork next month in New York."

"You know, Cate would be happy to take some of that off your hands, for the museum," said Michael.

Farber giggled, a high-pitched energetic laugh.

"Not a chance, Michael, not a chance. She's already taken one masterpiece."

"Drop in the bucket, so I hear," said Michael.

Farber sighed, but it seemed to Ramsgill more like she was feigning than offering a gesture that was sincere.

"Well, I suppose I should be going," she said. "I just wanted to say hello." She looked up at Ramsgill and smiled. "I do hope we meet again."

"Me too," said Ramsgill.

"I'll escort you out," said Michael. "My drink needs refreshing. Jamie? Elena?"

Ramsgill and Elena shook their heads then watched them walk away, Farber with a smile on her face that Ramsgill found slightly unsettling. He realized she was leaving the gallery for probably the last time. It was going to take her only weeks to dismantle her ex-husband's estate and move back home. There she would be out of the scrutinizing eyes of Dr. Farber's friends and relatives, free to spend his money as she wished.

Ramsgill turned back to the painting. He again found himself wondering what had prompted Farber to change his mind and leave it to the museum. He thought for a moment about Mrs. Addison and about her desire to keep the painting a secret. What would she think now, he wondered, to see it in a gallery.

"You can sort of see," he said to Elena, "how Mrs. Addison favored her mother. I mean I've only seen pictures of the two of them, but you can detect a definite resemblance in the way Eakins has portrayed Ms. Beecham. It just points out how good he was at detail."

Elena nodded, tucking a strand of hair behind an ear.

"Jamie, what was it Cate said about the chair in the painting? Something that helped corroborate its authenticity?"

"She said that because it was a Philadelphia chair, and one that seemed to have been in Eakins' estate, that it confirmed the real painting."

"What was that?" An older woman in a blue satin dress with a Chinese collar had overheard Ramsgill and was leaning forward toward the canvas, squinting through small eyes.

"The chair's design," Ramsgill said. "During the colonial period each city produced slight deviations in the carving of their furniture. See here?"

He stepped forward, pointing his little finger toward the chair in the foreground of the painting on which Ms. Beecham's clothes were draped. "Eakins was a stickler for detail and he was known to have owned a Chippendale chair from this period. It was supposed to have been carved by a Philadelphia furniture maker named Tuft. You can see it in the legs. Philadelphia chairs have these square rear legs."

"I beg your pardon?"

Another voice, deeper, that of a man came from just beyond the woman. A gray-haired gentleman wearing silver half-glasses was looking down at the chair in the picture.

"I said that these square rear legs differentiate the chair as being from Philadelphia. I think that if a chair is from New England, it has rounded legs. And something about these side rails. Philadelphia chairs have this straight type."

The man turned and looked at Ramsgill, peering from behind his glasses with skepticism.

"You have it wrong," he said. "It's the opposite. Philadelphia chairs have rounded rear legs and curved side rails. I should know. I curate furniture at Winterthur."

Ramsgill looked back at the canvas, wondering if the man was correct.

"I suppose you're right," he said. "But then why . . . ?"

He was sure that Cate had told him the real Eakins painting had a Philadelphia chair in it. He suddenly flashed to Hayes Chatfield, sitting in his wheelchair at the nursing home. Ramsgill tried to recall what he had said about the forged painting Mrs. Addison had brought to him. He had said that he knew intuitively it was a forgery, but also that his instincts were backed up by the fact that the chair had been different in Devero's forgery. It wasn't a Philadelphia chair. A Boston chair had been Devero's signature.

Just as it was on the painting before him.

"What's the matter, Jamie?"

Elena was looking at him strangely, and he realized his face was flush. He jerked his head in the direction of the hall, looking for Cate, for Claudia Farber, for anyone who knew more about the painting than he did.

And then it hit him.

It became perfectly clear, like the high, clean air of a Montana sky.

Fourteen

I have to find Cate," he said.

"But, Jamie, what is it?"

"I'll be back in a minute. Let me just see if she's out in the hall."

Ramsgill gave her his drink and hurried out of the gallery. By now the main hall was brimming with activity. More people had arrived, and the champagne had lubricated those already there. A cacophony of laughs and rising and falling voices lit the air. He looked for Cate and Claudia Farber, but all he could make out was an ocean of indistinguishable heads. He decided to climb the grand stair that led to the second floor, where he might be able to see clearer.

As he ascended, the music from the chamber ensemble, across the balcony toward the front of the museum, became louder. At the second landing of the stair he turned in front of Saint-Gaudens' huge bronze of *Diana*, and peered back down into the human mass below. Cate's auburn hair was nowhere to be seen. Nor was Farber's dress. He was just about to return downstairs when he caught Michael's eyes looking up at him.

Michael squinted, then craned his neck as if to ask the question, *What are you doing?* Jamie motioned with his hand for Michael to come up, and a moment later they were standing next to one another beneath the statue.

"What's up?" Michael said. "Come have a drink with me."

"No," said Jamie. "Something's wrong, Michael. With the Eakins painting. Where's Cate?"

"What's wrong with the painting?"

"Let's just find Cate. I'll tell you then. Have you seen her?"

"No, I—"

Just then, the two of them heard voices coming from one of the oversized doorways that led to the second floor galleries. A moment later Cate appeared with an elderly woman, the woman apparently quite comfortable with her, because she had her arm locked through Cate's. Cate was talking animatedly, and the woman, though old and infirm, was listening to her every word.

"Come on," said Jamie.

He started up the last flight of stairs, and they met Cate and the woman at the entrance to the Medieval and Renaissance galleries. A security guard in a gray uniform stood in the doorway.

"Cate," said Jamie, a sense of urgency in his voice. "Please. I need to talk to you."

Cate started to introduce the woman to Jamie and Michael, but Michael stopped her with a shake of his head.

"Okay," she said. "Mrs. Speake, I need to talk to these gentlemen." She turned toward the guard. "Robert, could you take Mrs. Speake back downstairs?"

The guard nodded and took the woman's arm. Cate said a polite good-bye, and they watched as the guard led her away.

"What is it?" she said, once they were gone. "Jamie, that woman is important to me. She has the country's largest collection of Charles Demuths, and she's thinking of donating them to the museum."

"Sorry," he said.

"Jamie says something's wrong with the Eakins," said Michael.

Cate's eyes narrowed, and her mouth became a hard, straight line. She looked out to the balcony. It ringed all sides of the upper story of the main hall, open in the middle down to below. Several couples were milling about the balcony opposite, listening to the chamber ensemble.

"Come in here," she said.

They turned and hurried through the opening, following her into a suite of galleries. They were period rooms comprised of columns, vaults, windows, doorways, floors, and other fragments of historic buildings, each in a different style. The walls of the rooms were hung with artwork from each period, and smaller side rooms were even more intimate in their decor. There was a Romanesque portal from the

Abbey of St. Laurent, a late-Gothic chapel, a small Dutch library. Shortly they came to a large, square room constructed of fragments of a medieval cloister, complete with surrounding walls of stucco, a tile roof, and marble columns and arches. Subtle cove lighting implied a high, dimly lit sky. In the middle of the courtyard was a Romanesque fountain, water trickling slowly from an ornate enclosure carved out of pink marble.

"Okay," she said. "What is it?"

Ramsgill looked to his sister-in-law. Her flaming waves of orange hair were pulled back tightly in a French braid. She wore a long, deep-green dress with a slit up one side. The color was a perfect complement to the hair, and her face was radiant, no doubt a reaction to the barrage of compliments she had been receiving all evening.

"The painting, Cate. It's a forgery."

Cate looked briefly to Michael. Jamie thought he actually saw her lip quiver as she turned her head back toward him. He thought of the evening, of the adulation that had been heaped upon her, of the fact that they wouldn't even be at the party had she not gotten the painting for the museum. This was undoubtedly the shining moment of her career, and here he was tearing her down.

"It has the wrong chair in it," he continued. "The day I saw it at your house, you pointed out to me how Eakins used a Philadelphia Chippendale chair in the painting. Right?"

She nodded.

"Well, Chatfield told me that one of the reasons he deemed Mrs. Addison's painting a forgery was that it had a Boston chair in it. The painting downstairs has a Boston chair in it."

"But I don't . . . " Cate hesitated. She again looked to Michael, who if he was worried about his wife's reputation, didn't seem to show it.

"Maybe you're wrong, Jamie," Michael said.

"I'm not, Michael. Cate, you've got to tell me. The morning after Farber died, you sent the painting back to Claudia Farber, right?"

"Yes," she said.

"You were at her house, Jamie," said Michael, "just after it arrived. Cate had a security firm take it back to her. At Pennwood."

Ramsgill paused, recalling the incidents of that morning.

"And you're sure that when it left your house, it was the real painting?" he said.

Cate spoke: "Of course I'm sure, Jamie."

Ramsgill shook off the irrationality of his thoughts, where this seemed to be taking him. He struggled to remember all that he knew about the painting, about the relationship between Dr. Farber, Laycutt, and Devero, about the blackmail letter, and about Claudia Farber. The inconsistencies kept pushing at him, like water leaking out of a sieve. There was no way he could hold it back.

"The blackmail letter was contrived," he said. "It was typed, it was unsigned, and the blackmailer had no assurances that by sending a letter instead of phoning Laycutt that it would ever arrive on time. It just doesn't make sense. And . . ." He suddenly remembered something. "Jesus, now I realize the return address was wrong. . . ."

"What?" Michael's voice floated upwards, trailing off like a train passing out of earshot.

"When I was trying to find out where Devero lived I telephoned the Jim Thorpe Post Office. They told me that Devero had a post office box, because he lived on a hill that was unserviceable in winter."

"So?"

"So it was odd enough that Devero would have put a return address on the envelope to begin with, much less one that was wrong. The envelope listed the return address as Forty-one Packer Avenue, not a P.O. box."

"Which means that Devero didn't write the letter?"

"Right. And that's not the only thing. Devero was not killed with a gun as Laycutt had intended. And remember? Laycutt told me he didn't go into the house."

"But what are you saying, Jamie?"

Ramsgill walked over to the fountain and dipped his fingers into the cool, oily water. He then turned back to them.

"I'm thinking that it's very odd that Claudia Farber is here tonight."

"Why?" said Cate. Her face was an ominous mask.

"She was not in love with her husband," said Ramsgill. "And she was shocked when Farber's secretary told her that she wasn't going to inherit the Eakins painting. Like you said, Michael, she can't wait to get out of the country."

"What?" said Michael. His thoughts seemed to be somewhere else.

Ramsgill removed his hands from the fountain and smoothed them on his dinner jacket.

"She's not a distraught woman," he said. "And don't you think that seeing the painting again would have stirred some emotion in her? You admitted that it's surprising she's here."

"Go on," said Cate.

"Farber and Laycutt had Devero paint the forgery," said Ramsgill. "And they made the switch for Mrs. Addison's real painting. They then waited until the forgery was declared a fake, and whether by design, or by luck, Farber bought the fake back from her. And why?"

"So he could destroy it," said Michael. "Thus, destroying any evidence of their crime."

"What if . . . ?" said Jamie.

He waited for Cate or Michael to prompt him. They didn't, so he continued. "What if . . . Farber didn't destroy it?"

"But why?"

"I don't know. To satisfy his ego. Whatever. But in any event Claudia finds the forgery."

"You mean after he's dead?"

"I suppose. I go to Pennwood the morning after he has died and I'm there when she finds out from Farber's secretary that he has bequeathed the painting to the museum. She's livid."

"But she has an out," said Michael.

"Yes," said Jamie. "She has the forgery. She can swap it for the real thing. Cate? Who looks at a painting when it comes to the museum, to ensure that it's genuine?"

"In this case," she said, "I did."

"But you didn't notice the chair?"

Again Cate looked at Michael.

"Well, no, Jamie. But that painting sat on my sideboard for four weeks. I know it like I know the back of my hand."

"But you didn't pick out the forger's signature."

"No. . . ."

Ramsgill looked at Cate's face carefully, almost as if it were under a microscope. The pores of her otherwise soft skin seemed to stand out against the paleness of her flesh, and her mouth and eyes twitched almost imperceptibly. She cast her gaze downward and brushed something away from the front of her dress, something that Ramsgill knew wasn't there.

She started to say something.

"Wha . . . ?" Jamie said. He purposefully left the word broken.

"What?" he said again.

"Nothing," said Cate.

"Are you sure?" he said. "Sure there's something I'm not missing?"

She looked up at him and swallowed, pulling in her lower lip.

"It wasn't Claudia Farber," he said. "Was it?"

"I don't understand," said Michael.

"Everything else fits," said Jamie. "Except for one thing."

Cate tilted her head to one side, implying a question. She was a beautiful woman, and it was unusual to see her in such pain.

"Claudia didn't know about her husband's codicil until the morning after he died," Ramsgill continued. "I learned from Vibeke Lidz that Farber had changed the will at the same time she did. And the threatened loss of the painting was Claudia's only conceivable motive. Why would she have killed him earlier, if she hadn't known about the codicil?"

Michael's eyes flashed at Jamie for a millisecond. Jamie stepped back from the fountain, his own eyes not leaving his brother. He felt gutted, like a fish that has had its insides ripped out by a fisherman only to be thrown back into the water. He looked up at the smooth Romanesque arches and shadows of the cloister and recalled, almost as if the memory were a missile boring its way into his heart, something from his childhood.

"Michael," he said coolly, "do you remember the day you left home? When you left Mother and me and moved in with Dad?"

Michael's round face was impassive, a slight glistening of sweat on his forehead reflecting under the lights.

"You were sixteen. I was eight. I got home from school that day and Mom sat me down. She let me have a 7-Up float, and I knew right then something was wrong because she hardly ever let us have sweets. I can still remember what she was wearing. It was that light blue seersucker smock, the one with the star on the pocket, and her hair was short back then. After finishing my float I remember asking her where you were, because I had learned at school that day that Jackie Robinson had just been elected to the Hall of Fame. Mom said that you had left us, that you were going to live with Dad. I started crying, and she held me close, and I stayed there for what must have been an hour. Then she told me to go lie down, that she'd bring me dinner in bed. I didn't want to lie down, I didn't want to do anything. I remember feeling like I had been split in half. Half of me was Mother's, half of me was yours and Dad's." He paused, noticing that Michael's sweat was building. "But that changed when I got to my room. I found my Phillies baseball bank, the one Granddad had given me for my sixth birthday, on my bed. It was cracked open and most of my money was gone. I must have had twenty-five dollars in there, money from my newspaper route. You had taken it."

Jamie looked up to his brother, glaring at him. They stood there motionless, as if they were icebergs separated by a cold, dark, arctic sea. Jamie then turned and started walking back towards the main hall of the museum.

"What are you doing?" Michael said, running to catch up with him at the edge of the cloister.

"I'm going to phone the police," Ramsgill mumbled.

"Stop, Jamie. Talk to us. Tell us what's happening."

He turned and tried to look Michael in the eye, but Michael skirted his gaze.

"I was foolishly thinking it was Claudia Farber," Jamie said. Cate now stood behind Michael, her pitiful head against the arm of his tuxedo jacket. "But it wasn't. I remember something now from when I was attacked at Devero's. My attacker left with an object, an object which I've been thinking all along was another briefcase. But it wasn't a briefcase. It was something wrapped in brown paper. And it was flat, tucked under his arm. *His* arm. A man's arm."

"So?"

"So there were Eakins items in the garage. The maquettes. The photographs of the real painting. Why would a man keep that out in his studio for twenty years? The answer is that he wouldn't. Those things were laid out for a purpose. But what it really boils down to is the missing twenty-five thousand dollars. I now realize that there wasn't any missing money. In actuality there were two sets of money. The codicil to Farber's will was just the last piece to fall in place."

"What do you mean, 'the last piece'? " said Michael. "It was Laycutt."

"Wrong," said Jamie. "Someone else showed up at Devero's door that night, shortly before I got there. It was the person who wrote the blackmail note. The purpose of the note was to get Laycutt and Devero together so they could be disposed of. But the blackmailer came under other pretensions."

"What pretensions?"

"The pretension of having Devero paint a new facsimile. They brought a briefcase with fifty thousand dollars to buy it. That's why there appeared to be a discrepancy in the money. Why the Eakins stuff was out in the garage studio. And Devero was killed facing one of his paintings. He was engaged in conversation with someone, showing them his work. Perhaps someone who had never seen it. Do you think if Laycutt had been the killer, he would have done that? Their meeting would hardly have been amicable. And the killer left with something under his arm."

"Another painting?"

"Yes. Another facsimile. Devero never blackmailed anyone, just like his sister said. The person who bought the new facsimile did it. And that same person killed Farber."

"But why?"

Ramsgill swallowed, his saliva glands now gushing like the open spillway of a dam.

"Cate, why didn't you tell me that Farber was leaving the painting to the museum when you first learned that I was working for Farr?"

"I don't know, Jamie. We'd just gotten the codicil. I suppose it slipped my mind."

"Who executed the codicil?"

Cate's eyes rose to Michael.

"I thought so. As Turner Baltzell said earlier, it helps if a curator has a lawyer for a husband. You two knew Farber had the real painting and you somehow knew that Devero had made them a forgery twenty years ago. You got Devero to make you another one. But before you did, you told Farber that you knew of his plot. You threatened to expose him unless he bequeathed the painting to the museum. He signed the codicil, which no one knew about except for Michael and yourself. Then you killed him. With both the painting and the forgery, you then kept the real painting for yourself. You sent the forgery to Claudia Farber. After probate, the forgery came into the collection of the museum. And as you were the only person at the museum to examine it upon accession, you could claim it was genuine. You are made curator, and somewhere at home you have six or seven million dollars' worth of pigment and cloth."

"Jamie, this is preposterous," said Michael. "I didn't kill anyone. Listen, I was at my office the night Devero died. Remember?"

"You said you were at your office. But I called there from upstate and was told you weren't in. If you really had that merger deadline, then you wouldn't have left."

"But, no. Come on . . ."

"You come on. You had plenty of time after killing Devero to get home before I did. But first you called the Jim Thorpe police. What were you thinking? Pin the murder on your brother. Let him take the rap."

"No. You're talking nonsense, Jamie."

"Bullshit, Michael. And then when I got back to your house and told you what had happened, you wanted me to turn myself in."

"I just wanted you to clear your name. I didn't want—"

"No more lies, Michael."

Cate let go of Michael's arm and walked drearily back into the cloister. She collapsed on a low stone wall that faced the fountain, her eyes watery, her face ashen. Water dripping from the fountain filled the room with a tortuous sound.

"This is my favorite spot," she said weakly, "In the whole museum. Sometimes I come here in the middle of the day. I just sit and imagine that I'm in France, and it's the thirteenth century. My job, the city, it's out there somewhere, but I don't care. In here, it's nothing but solitude."

"How did you know about the forgery?" said Jamie.

Cate looked up at him longingly, eager, it seemed, to get the weight of what they had done off her chest.

"The same way you did," she said. "I knew Hayes Chatfield was too much of a connoisseur to have been wrong in calling the painting a forgery if it wasn't. He told me enough to get my curiosity aroused, then we confronted Farber. He told us the whole story, and all about Devero. And you're right, Devero knew nothing. But you've got to believe me, Jamie, murder was never something I had planned. That was all Michael."

She looked over to her husband, fear and deep hurt in her swollen eyes.

"I just wanted the real painting for the museum," she continued. "And besides, it wasn't legally Farber's. I was caught up in the euphoria of the idea, thinking selfishly that it would insure my promotion. That's all Michael told me we were going to do."

"What was your plan, Michael?" Jamie asked. "Were you going to sell it on the black market?"

Michael wouldn't look at him. He just stared at the wall.

"Who's Arthur Goldstein?" Jamie said. Again, no answer, no look.

"He was a client of Michael's," said Cate.

"Shut up," said Michael.

"He's suing you," said Jamie. "I saw the complaint in your kitchen the night Devero was murdered. Is that it? How much is he suing you for? And why?"

"Three million dollars," said Cate. "Michael represented Goldstein's company in a leveraged buyout. But the deal fell through and Goldstein says it was Michael's fault. Even if Micheal settles, it will cost a lot of money."

"Shut up, Cate," Michael repeated. He walked over to her and, from nowhere, brought a hand sharply across her face. She began to cry in short sharp bursts, not unlike the bray of a donkey. Jamie grabbed Michael by the shoulders, pulling him away from her. They wrestled until Jamie had pinned him against a pillar.

"Stop it!" Michael cried, his arms flailing like a marionette, trying to get a hand on Jamie. Jamie grabbed him again, then shoved him to the floor.

"This time I can see you," Jamie said. "And you don't have a briefcase."

Michael started to stand, his eyes burning, his mouth in a grimace.

"Don't get up," Jamie warned. "I swear, Michael, I'll kill you."

Michael stayed down, bringing the rear of his hand across his mouth. Blood now seeped from its corner, matching the color of his vest.

"For three months I've been thinking that I was wrong about you, Michael. But now, I realize that your killing Laycutt had nothing to do with me. You probably wouldn't have minded if he'd killed me first. You would have still shot him, because that was the only way to protect this sordid scheme. You're sick. You're going to prison and you are going to rot there."

"I didn't want to hurt you, Jamie."

"Well, you have."

Cate began to cry again and Michael slid over to her. She jerked away.

"I had no idea it would lead to murder," she blurted between sobs. "Jamie, you have to believe that! It was stupid. I told him there was

162

no way to put a forgery into the museum. That we'd be caught immediately."

She looked up at him, her face convulsing in tears.

"This is so terrible," she cried. "Our lives are ruined. Michael, how could you have killed them? How could you? How . . . !"

Michael grabbed her mouth between his massive hand and squeezed hard. She reeled back in pain.

"Leave her alone!"

Jamie pried Michael's hand away. Cate gasped for breath. Ramsgill felt sorry for her, even though he knew he shouldn't. He wanted to protect her from Michael, perhaps in a way that he himself had never been protected. He took her by the hand and pulled her up.

She looked down at her husband.

"You even sent somebody after Jamie," she said. "To kill him."

"Not to kill him," said Michael. "To scare him."

Michael looked up defiantly, but this time it was Jamie who looked away. Jamie looked down at him. Michael just went into himself, pulling his legs up to his chest, his arms wrapping them. He was crying now. Jamie couldn't recall ever having heard him cry.

Jamie put his arm around Cate's cold, bare shoulder, and slowly led her to the door, then through the adjacent galleries, finally coming to the balcony portal. He looked back once, but could hear nothing.

At the balcony Ramsgill turned left and led her to the stairs. As they reached the landing beneath the statue of Diana, they turned again. Like a frail debutante in the arms of her chaperone, Cate clung to Jamie's arm. Her dress was resplendent, though the green velvet was now peppered with tears. Below them the crowd had swelled, and in the far corner of the hall Ramsgill could see Elena looking up at them. Suddenly, he heard the sound of clapping, at first a single pair of hands, but followed by several more, then a multitude. At the base of the stair Turner Baltzell was standing next to Mrs. Speake, clapping furiously and smiling as he looked up to the new curatorial star of his museum.

Cate buried her head into Jamie's shoulder just as Jamie had once buried his into his mother's chest. She wasn't going to go out in style, the way Norma Desmond did in the final scene of *Sunset Boulevard*. She cowered at the applause. Ramsgill responded by wrapping her shoulders tightly within his arms, careful to lead her feet to each subsequent step as they descended. At long last they came to the bottom of the stair, and without comment, at first Baltzell, and then others stepped back to give Jamie and Cate a path through the crowd. Cate's eyes were blank now, and as the sea of people before them split apart, she hardly noticed. When they reached the far end of the room, he set her limp body down in a chair, adjacent to the museum's information desk. Her head flopped over, and he used his body to hold her up the best he could. He reached over the desk and picked up the telephone's receiver. He dialed the operator and asked for the police.

Cate's tenure as curator of American Art was over, ending as auspiciously as it had begun.

Fifteen

*J*amie, will you answer it?"

Jamie Ramsgill was teetering atop an aluminum ladder, one foot clinging to the next to last rung, the other hanging out in space. An arm was stretched far to his left, smoothing out a wide joint of drywall compound with a joint knife.

For four weeks now it had been like this, and Ramsgill was beginning to wonder if they were insane. He and Elena had moved into their new home, though *moved into* was a relative term. The place was under construction—a collage of unfinished partitions, stacks of metal studs, boxes of unopened and uninstalled light fixtures, bundles of wood flooring, new kitchen cabinets scattered about like a tornado had blown through the place. *Home* was relative too. They had bought a derelict grain warehouse just north of the Ben Franklin Parkway and were converting its tower into living quarters.

"Jamie, please!"

Ramsgill now realized that the phone was ringing. He looked across the raw space and saw that Elena Piruzzi was in a worse state than he was. She too was atop a ladder, with a long strip of wet wallpaper draped over her, a scowl planted firmly on her lips.

"Let it ring!" he called. "It's probably Michael's firm again. Or worse yet, the press."

The ringing didn't stop. Reluctantly, Ramsgill wiped a glob of wet joint compound from his forearm and scrambled down to the concrete floor. He hurried toward the sound of the phone, which was somewhere in the vicinity of a pile of sheet-metal ductwork.

He didn't want to talk to the press. He had tried to block out the news reports of his brother's arrest, and most of the memory of what Michael had done. In the end, ironically, it was the blocking out that hurt him the most. The only way to live with the fact that his brother had killed three people was to erase what had happened. But for Ramsgill that also meant expunging all memories of Michael, even the good ones. His method of coping had been to simply rewind his memory back to childhood and pretend that Michael had just left home.

After that, his indifference became easier. It made it possible to refuse to help Michael's law firm when they called, asking that he be a character witness for Michael's bail hearing. He refused to be interviewed by the press or to acknowledge any relationship at all to Michael Ramsgill.

Ramsgill finally located the cordless phone. He set down his compound knife and picked up the handset.

"Hello."

"Hello? This is Bernice Devero. Is Mr. Ramsgill there?"

Ramsgill let the voice sink in.

"Mr. Ramsgill? It's me. Bernice."

"Oh . . . Ms. Devero. I'm sorry."

"I'm at Major's house," she went on. "Like you said. The phone don't work here, but the real estate lady, she's letting me use her flip phone. She's in kind of a hurry, so she said if I'd just get what it was that I'd come for, she got to be going on her way."

"Yes," said Ramsgill. "That's nice of her."

"The reason I called," said Bernice, "is that I don't see nothing behind the refrigerator, that's for sure."

"The refrigerator?" said Ramsgill. He now remembered their discussion from before. "I didn't say refrigerator. I said dryer. It's in a utility closet in the back hallway."

He wondered if he was right, if the money would really be there. After Laycutt was killed the newspapers had reported that the blackmail money had been recovered. They didn't say from where, but Ramsgill had assumed they had found it at Devero's. It wasn't until later, when Ramsgill realized that there had been *two* sets of money, that he had begun to wonder. After all, there had been no mention in the press of any money having been found in Jim Thorpe. Michael's fifty thousand. Certainly, if a second set of money had been found, it would have raised suspicion. Once Ramsgill realized what had happened, he thought about bringing it to the attention of the police. But then, impulsively, he had another idea.

If he told them about the fifty thousand at Devero's house, it would become the state's evidence and be kept in limbo for months, if not years, as Michael would no doubt put up the best murder defense that his wealth could muster. Even if Michael was convicted and the money used as partial remuneration to the families of the victims, it would be a long time before Bernice Devero would see a penny of it.

She didn't have years. Her boy Daryl was growing up fast. Ramsgill couldn't put the image of their row house, and the street on which they lived, out of his mind. Daryl would be a teenager before Bernice could blink, faced with survival in the Badlands. Fifty thousand dollars wasn't going to take care of all of her problems, but it would get her a house somewhere else in the city.

"I've found it!" It was Bernice again, panting over the phone line. "It was right where you said. Thank goodness Daryl's little old arm would fit down in there. He pulled it out for me."

For the first time in weeks Ramsgill actually felt good about something.

"Now, listen," he said. "First of all, don't dare open that briefcase in front of the real estate agent. As far as she knows, it contains some old family mementos. Bring it back to the city. Take five hundred dollars for Daryl and yourself, then open five separate bank accounts at downtown banks. Each of the new accounts should be opened for less than ten thousand. That way nothing gets reported. No neighborhood banks, and for God's sake don't take the money back to North Philly with you. In a week or so you'll be able to write checks on your new accounts. Start looking for a house, and don't get greedy. There's no need to spend the whole fifty thousand. If you can find a place in a good neighborhood for less, buy it. I'll make sure that you eventually get a settlement from my brother. But that's going to take some time."

He could hear her starting to cry.

"Bernice, don't. You don't want the real estate agent to suspect anything."

"It's all right," she said. "She's out in the yard. But I am sitting here running up her phone bill."

"You better go then. Good luck."

Ramsgill heard a sniffle, and then she spoke again.

"God bless you, Mr. Ramsgill."

"It's Jamie," he said. "And I didn't do a thing. This is money your brother was owed. I only wish I could erase what happened to him."

"Still," she said. "Thank you."

Ramsgill hung up the phone gingerly, reconstituting a silent solitude in his mind. He glanced back toward the open kitchen and smiled, seeing that Elena had gotten her wallpaper to behave. He then stepped around the ductwork and made his way over to a wall of steel sash windows, thirty feet of nothing but city, eight stories below and stretching out as far as the eye could survey. Their penthouse, when finished, would be spectacular. It was almost dusk, and the skyline was beginning to glow like the embers of some gigantic dying fire. The slender silhouette of David Laycutt's Keystone Place distinguished itself from the rest of downtown's towers, unglazed as of yet, no glass to reflect the waning sunlight. Two twinkling red lights capped its dark steel frame, and if Ramsgill suspended belief, he could almost see them as the crazed loathsome eyes of his friend Laycutt, just as he had come for Jamie on Belmont Plateau.

Elena slipped silently up behind him; he flinched when she put a tender hand on his shoulder, his thoughts focused on Laycutt. He turned and gave her a longing look. The scent of her body was sweeter than honeysuckle, and it rose above the medley of construction smells. He cradled the back of her head with his fingers and pulled her to his open lips. They kissed once, and then a second time.

"Who was on the phone?" she asked.

"The phone? Nobody. Just some woman soliciting donations."

"You didn't give her anything, did you?"

"Yeah. Fifty thousand dollars."

Elena laughed, her eyes looking up at him like two magnets, drawing him in, holding him tight.

"I'm glad you got your sense of humor back," she said.

He lightly brushed her cheek with his hand.

"About ready to break for dinner?" she asked.

Ramsgill looked toward the kitchen, now almost wallpapered, but with rough plumbing lines poking up through the concrete slab, wires dangling from holes in the walls. The kitchen cabinets were still in boxes, weeks away from being installed.

"What'd you cook up?" he said. "A little wallpaper paste soup?"

"We can go out," she said.

"We can go out?" he said. "Like we have a choice?"

"Or we can stay in."

He pulled her to him, her warmth enveloping him like a blanket.

"And eat what?" he said.

She gave him a goofy grin, then replied, "Use your imagination."

"You are naughty, Ms. Piruzzi."

"I've had a good teacher."

He tugged at her cheek, then lifted her up, stepping over a box. As he carried her across the room, he tried to remember where they had stashed the bed.